WHAT KILLED ROSIE?

An
Emily Menotti
Mystery

by

MARYELLEN WINKLER

Also by Maryellen Winkler:

The Disappearance of Darcie Malone

Cruising to Death

ISBN
978-1-935751-30-4 (paperback)
978-1-935751-28-1 (eBook)

Published by
Scribbulations LLC
Kennett Square, Pennsylvania
U.S.A.

This is a work of fiction. Names, characters, places, and incidents either are the product of the author's imagination or are used fictitiously, and any resemblance to any actual persons, living or dead, events, or locales is entirely coincidental.

*This book is dedicated to my dad,
who first inspired me by reading
story poems to me at a very early age,
and to my mom, who created those
quiet evenings so necessary
for storytelling.*

Acknowledgments

I want to thank my dear friend, Donna Moe, who volunteered to be my first-look editor, and Grace Spampinato, who offered wonderful support and advice.

Chapter One: May 2000

"Meet me at the Laundromat at seven thirty this evening," my neighbor, Jackie, said. "My laundry should be ready for the dryer by then. We'll have an hour to grab a bite to eat."

So at 7:25 p.m. I left the small, white frame home that I share with my boyfriend and started down Elm Street to meet my neighbor. It was one of those soft spring nights in New Hampshire that you wish would go on forever—no harsh sun, no stinging rain, just the warm caress of the evening air.

The approach from Elm Street brings one to the rear of the Laundromat. When I was about a block away, I saw a figure emerge from the back door. She paused under the solitary bulb hanging over the entry, the only point of light in the gathering dusk of the evening.

The woman carried a plastic basket brimming with clothes. As I approached, I could see that it wasn't Jackie. This figure was older and had brownish, rather than pale blonde, hair. The woman whose features were becoming distinct looked bizarrely familiar.

She paused for a moment beneath the halo of light. When I got close enough to see her clearly, what I saw took my breath away. I was looking at my friend, Rosie, who had been dead for five years.

I started to run, half-stumbling over the broken pavement. I had to get closer; I had to find out who this person was.

Then my foot caught a wayward tree root and I fell, smashing my chin on the cement. Dazed, I pushed myself up to a sitting position. I looked for the woman in the doorway. She was gone.

I sat there for a few moments, dabbing at a bit of blood on my chin and feeling foolish for falling. When I picked myself up, I went inside the Laundromat and saw Jackie, pulling her clothes from the washing machine. I asked about the woman with dark hair that I'd seen in the doorway.

"What woman?" she replied. "There's no one here but me."

CHAPTER TWO: MAY 1995

The red light was blinking on my phone to let me know I had a message. The meeting I'd just been released from had been overly long and boring to boot. In my opinion, Corporate America would get a lot more done with a lot fewer meetings.

Luckily, I had decided to check my messages before I went to lunch. The message was from my friend, Rosie, who'd recently turned forty-seven.

"I'm not feeling too well," she said. She was using her little-girl voice, the voice that frightened me. "My chest hurts. Can you come and take me to the emergency room?"

I lit out of work as fast as I could and drove the 2.3 miles to her home. Because the message had been left forty minutes earlier, I prayed I wasn't too late.

I had a key to her apartment so I could feed her cats whenever she traveled. I knocked first and then went in, leaving the door ajar in case I needed to exit quickly and get help.

The apartment was dark and eerily quiet. I went down the short hallway to the living room. Rosie was sprawled on her back, as motionless as a doll dropped on the living room rug.

Rosie's red silk dressing gown spread around her like seeping blood. Her brown hair was disheveled as if she'd just got out of bed. Her mouth gaped wide, and her eyes were open but seeing nothing. She was very pale, very still.

I got on my knees beside her and put two fingers on her carotid artery, feeling for a pulse. There was none. Then I put my right ear slightly above her mouth to listen and feel for a breath. Again, there was none. I needed to call for help.

I went to the tiny kitchen and called 9-1-1, explaining that Rosie wasn't breathing. The operator understood immediately. She asked the address and then reassured me an ambulance was on the way. She then asked if I knew CPR, and I replied that I did. She suggested I return to Rosie and begin CPR immediately.

I don't know how I was able to remain so calm and remember the rescue ABC's: Airway, Breathing, Chest Compression.

I checked her airway first, swirling my fingers around her mouth to remove any obstructions. There were none. Then I listened again for her breath. Nothing.

I blew a breath into her, then I placed my hands together in the middle of her chest and pressed down. I'd never done this outside of a classroom, and I'd no idea if I was doing it correctly now, but I had to do something until help arrived. I tried to concentrate on counting and on my hands creating just the right amount of pressure. It's a bit like kneading bread, only faster and harder. All the while I stared at Rosie's face, hoping for a miracle.

In only minutes my arms were aching, but I hung in until the ambulance came screaming up the road. Then I heard the EMTs running through the apartment building's front door and stomping up the stairs to Rosie's. They praised my quick action as they took over.

I was surprised at how slowly and deliberately they worked. I'd expected them to barge in and whisk Rosie off with sirens blaring. Instead, they carefully listened for her breath and checked her mouth as I had done.

"No pulse," said a man in a navy windbreaker with Swansea Fire Department emblazoned in red thread on the back.

"I think there's a faint heartbeat," said a burly young blonde woman in a similar jacket holding a stethoscope to Rosie's chest. "I'm not sure."

While they were working on her, they asked me if I knew if she had taken any drugs or harmed herself in anyway. I answered that I didn't think so. Then they brought out the paddles and told me to stand back.

They shocked her three times. Each time her chest barely moved, unlike the dramatic heaves you see in the movies.

"Still no pulse," said the man.

"Let's take her then," the woman said.

"Is she dead?" I asked as they placed her on the stretcher.

"We don't know," she replied, but I had the sinking feeling that if she wasn't dead now, Rosie would be shortly. The hospital would only confirm it.

I followed the ambulance to the hospital, hoping that, in the absence of next of kin, they'd tell me why she died. Rosie had lost both her parents; her brief marriage had yielded no children. She had cut off her only sister claiming that Michelle was too selfish. Over the years she had pretty much jettisoned all her friends and family for one imagined wrong or another. I don't know how I'd been allowed to stay.

My thoughts floundered, adrift in a sea of medical and legal issues I was unfamiliar with. I had no idea how to contact her sister. The hospital staff would have to figure that out. I didn't have a power of attorney. In the event that they couldn't save her, I guessed my only responsibility would be to take her cats to the SPCA.

The emergency waiting room could have been in any hospital in the western world. Molded plastic seats or arm chairs with Naugahyde backs and cushions were scattered around the room. A gray Formica cabinet and countertop offered a coffee pot and Styrofoam cups along with the inevitable powdered cream, fake and real sugars, and tea bags. Standing next to the cabinet was a Poland Springs water dispenser. A few *People* magazines from last year lay on a wood corner table. I was too upset to drink coffee or read a magazine. I sat down and waited for news.

One of the many wonders of hospitals is that, amid all the institutional chairs and tables, beautiful paintings often adorn the walls, usually coffee-table book scenes of pink dogwoods in spring or snow-covered barns in winter. I sat on a squeaky Naugahyde chair and contemplated the beauty of the New Hampshire countryside, trying not to imagine the worst about Rosie.

After waiting about forty minutes, a young Asian doctor came in and, as I was the only one there, walked directly over to me and smiled at me sadly but sympathetically.

"I'm Doctor Singh," he said. "I'm sorry to tell you that your friend has died. Her heart sustained too much damage. We couldn't save her."

He was eye level with me; his dark eyes were kind. His straight black hair was longish and combed back from his face. I wondered if there were a Mrs. Singh waiting for him somewhere or if the wedding wouldn't happen until his residency was over. Was she his choice or his parents? Odd what you think about at the most inappropriate moments.

"Thank you for speaking to me. Can I see Rosie and say good-bye?"

"Of course. Go through these double doors here and go down the hall to room 29A, on your right. I'll come and talk to you there in a few minutes."

The doors squeaked softly as I pushed through them. The linoleum was pale ivory and shining, lighting my way as I quietly walked down the sterile white corridor to a swinging wooden door with the brass markings 29A.

Once inside, I was at first taken aback by the array of machines, maybe four of five, spread out on either side of the hospital bed. They blinked with red and blue lights, advertising illustrated graphs with flat green lines. After my initial shock, I noticed that none were hooked up to the figure beneath the sheet. Their sullen presence was like gangsters at a funeral — omens of the horrors that can befall the poor, fallible human body.

I pulled back the sheet covering her face. Her eyes were closed and her mouth slack; there was a total absence of expression. Again, an inappropriate thought flashed through my mind: Rosie has left the building. I hoped the ghost of Elvis would forgive me the comparison.

I couldn't bring myself to kiss her farewell, not even on the forehead. As friends, we'd never kissed, not even on the cheek. Instead, I held her lifeless hand. Instinctively, I tried to warm it with both of mine. There would be no warming.

"Good-bye," I whispered. "Sleep well."

I was startled by Dr. Singh appearing at my side.

"What happens now?" I asked.

The hospital staff would try to find her next of kin, he said. St. Agnes of the Veil was the only hospital in town, and they were sure to have previously obtained that information if Rosie had ever been there before.

I thanked him again for his kindness and tiptoed out of the room. I found my way down the empty corridor and followed the exit signs until I was outside again and across from the parking lot. I took my time walking to my car.

Rosie's sudden death didn't seem quite right to me. Her parents had both lived into their eighties. I'd never heard her mention a family history of heart disease. As far as I knew, she was in good health.

By now it was late afternoon, and I was too shaken up to return to work. So I went home and called in and simply said I had left work because I felt sick. I got out my photo albums and looked at happy snaps of the two of us out to dinner with her coworkers or half-drunk with champagne on New Year's Eve. We'd only been friends for five years, but there were a lot of good times to remember.

The next day, after I'd taken the cats to an animal shelter and resisted the temptation to go through her personal effects, I contacted the hospital again but was told firmly that their privacy policy prohibited their giving me any further information about Rosie's death or the whereabouts of her family.

Two weeks later I got a note in the mail from Michelle Davenport, Rosie's sister.

Michelle didn't explain how she'd learned of Rosie's death, so I assumed the hospital had her name on file as next of kin. She did explain that she'd found my name in Rosie's address book, the only name not crossed out with strong black X's.

Michelle thanked me for seeing that Rosie was taken to a hospital. She wanted me to know that she had arranged to have her body cremated, and that Rosie had left all her money to the SPCA. That was it; there was no return address, no phone number. Perhaps, like Rosie, she too had limited success with friendships.

It seemed too sudden an end to a five-year relationship that had been marked by many good times as well as bad, like the times Rosie had had altercations with local merchants and highway patrolmen or had been angry with me.

I'd have liked to raise my concerns to Michelle about Rosie's good health and the odds of her dying of a heart attack at forty-seven, but I had no way to contact her. There was nothing else do.

Over the following months, I continued to miss Rosie terribly. I would read about a good movie or a new restaurant, think of calling Rosie, and then realize she couldn't join me. I'd have a funny dream or a bad day at work and want to share it, and then remember she was gone.

She'd been my only real woman friend since I'd moved to New Hampshire with my former husband over five years ago. I had chosen instead to stay close to old friends from my native Delaware through weekly phone calls and occasional visits home.

In time, I only thought of Rosie on the odd occasion when I passed a restaurant she'd liked or the hairdresser she'd frequented. When I thought of the circumstances of her death, it all seemed a terribly anonymous way to depart what had been a rather colorful life. Who was I to question a doctor? But I never felt completely sure that they'd got it right.

CHAPTER THREE: MAY 2000

When I arrived home that evening, my boyfriend immediately noticed the cut on my chin and the distracted look in my eyes. I had barely gotten my jacket off when he handed me a glass of Pinot Grigio. There was a concerned expression in his pale baby-blues.

"Do you need a Band-Aid?" he asked.

I told him I'd be fine.

Bud was a retired police detective whom I'd met back in February when pursuing the disappearance of a young girl named Darcie Malone. He'd helped me solve the mystery by introducing me to one of the witnesses. With just a little verbal pushing, we were able to persuade her to tell the truth about what had happened the night Darcie vanished.

I remember thinking that the police had dropped the ball in Darcie's case and hadn't investigated as thoroughly as they should have back in 1969. But on the other hand, as it turned out, no one would have been prosecuted anyway.

As a result of our meeting and my liking his Hemingway good looks, I accepted when Bud asked me out. As we dated, he showed himself to be such a gentleman and a genuinely caring person that I put aside my doubts about his previous job performance. Besides, he'd been a rookie back in 1969. The officers that he reported to could have been the ones to let the disappearance slide.

The end result was that after a few months of dating, many wonderful weekends at his seaside cottage in Portsmouth, numerous delicious home-cooked meals (which he cooked), and several games of penny-ante poker (which he let me win), I invited him to move in with me.

At fifty-one, knowing relationships at this age could end abruptly for many reasons—Rosie's unexpected death was one such example—and never being afraid of a calculated risk in the romance department, I was only too glad to empty a bureau drawer for Bud's underwear and socks and condense my wardrobe to half the closet. Bud kept his apartment which, considering the newness of our relationship, was the prudent thing to do.

I never regretted his moving in. He transformed my impersonal little bungalow into a celebration of life. Now when I arrived home, instead of entering dim, cold rooms aching for human warmth, I heard Fleetwood Mac on the stereo, was delighted to see fresh flowers on the kitchen table, was handed a glass of wine, and was told to sit and relax while Bud and I discussed our day.

Bud favored golf shirts and khaki shorts winter and summer, all worn with Teva sandals. I don't think he felt the cold at all. Although he wore a jacket in winter, rarely did he don gloves or a hat. I often wondered if he had some weather-resistant Nordic blood in his ancestry. He claimed not, but who could know for sure?

His thick white hair, longish and smooth, gave him a sporty look. Quick-witted, he could hold up his end of any conversation. Despite an extra forty pounds or so on his six-foot-five frame, he was still attractive enough to turn the heads of women of all ages when he walked into a room.

Perhaps the most touching thing about Bud, however, was his relationship with his golden retriever. There has never been, and to my mind never will be, a dog more patient and loving than Bud's dog Casey. They had been inseparable since Casey's adoption from a rescue shelter ten years earlier, so when Bud moved in, Casey came too. He was a welcome replacement for my cat, Zoe, who had disappeared a month earlier.

Accompanied by much barking and tail wagging, Bud and I made our way to the living room where we sat down and put our feet up. Then I told him about my encounter with Rosie. While he poured himself a martini, he told me he didn't believe in ghosts and omens and all that hogwash. I'd simply seen someone who resembled Rosie and who'd probably gotten into a waiting car that took off before I recovered from my fall.

I knew what I had seen and it was Rosie, but I wasn't going to argue with him. Bud was not a person open to paranormal experiences, despite his assistance with my search for Darcie.

He asked me about Rosie, and I told him about her unexpected heart attack. He said that in his experience as a police officer, the forties were a dangerous time to have one.

He explained that having a heart attack in your sixties or so, you may have already built up extra arteries around your heart to relieve the pressure that accumulates with age. The process resembled building side roads to relieve the congestion of a busy highway. Because of this, by sixty you were more likely to survive a heart event. In your thirties and forties, the side roads were not completed.

I told him about her parents living until their eighties and he just said there was no way of knowing why Rosie's heart had been vulnerable. She may have had rheumatic fever as a child or any number of illnesses that could have left a heart weak and damaged.

After I changed into my comfy sweats, I brought the topic up again. As Bud poured himself another martini and me a second glass of wine, I told him what little I knew of her life and, again, how perplexed I was at her sudden death without any warning signs of heart disease. Bud dismissed it all as part of the many mysteries of life and death that he couldn't be bothered to ponder. I didn't argue with him, but I decided I would look into it a little more on my own.

Chapter Four: Saturday

The next morning was a Saturday. As I did every morning, I rose before Bud and did a fifteen minute yoga workout. I loved starting the day with the Sun Salutation, stretching up to the sky with my hands touching in prayer, then bending down to the earth with my hands now touching my toes. This exercise made my back feel so good.

Then there were deep breaths and balancing postures, followed by my getting down on the floor to slowly glide through the positions of Cobra, Locust, and Swan. I finished with the Child, kneeling on the floor and sitting on my calves with my arms outstretched before me. My hope was that these exercises would keep both my brain and my body as healthy and youthful as possible.

After showering and dressing for the day, I usually had a bowl of cereal. Bud wasn't much for breakfast, but breakfast was my credo. So I usually made Bud an English muffin and brought it up to him so we could eat breakfast together in bed. When we were done eating, we sipped coffee together and watched the news.

Next Bud and I pursued our usual weekend chores of grocery shopping and taking his car to be washed and vacuumed. When we were done, I suggested we stop by the Laundromat and I'd show a photo of Rosie to anyone who was there in case they could identify the Rosie look-alike I'd seen.

On our way to the laundry, we drove up and down Swansea's narrow streets, slowly motoring beneath the green canopy of trees that shaded white shingled homes. Each home had green or black shutters and a three-foot band of red aluminum on the lower roof that encouraged the snow to melt.

Swansea, New Hampshire, had become my adopted home after my husband and I moved here ten years earlier. The springs were baby-soft and warm, the falls sour apple crisp, and the summers a hazy afternoon nap of golden sunlight dancing on the dusky blue surface of its many lakes and rivers. My husband eventually left, but I stayed.

The town sits at the junction of Routes 9 and 10, roads that can take you to Concord, New Hampshire; Brattleboro, Vermont; or along a patchwork of other routes to Maine and Massachusetts. Swansea was granted a charter by the New Hampshire governor in 1735 and, because of its location on the Severn River, was originally planned as a river fort to guard the Provence of Massachusetts Bay at the time of the French and Indian Wars. During that conflict, Swansea was burned to the ground by the Indians, but stalwart settlers managed to rebuild it during the 1760s. It survived and prospered, aided by the fierce rapids of the Severn River, which provided excellent power for cotton mills and other industries.

When my husband left me to farm the greener pastures of younger women, I chose to stay in New Hampshire and managed to survive the bone-chilling winters and heavy snows. Eventually, I not only survived, but grew strong and self-sufficient. Who needs a gym when a hundred inches of snow can fall on your front walk in one year? Although the neighbors might have still considered me a newcomer after ten years, I felt this was my home.

When we pulled up in front of the laundry, Queene Cleane II, Bud said he'd wait in the car with Casey. I figured he wouldn't have to wait long since, from the outside, it appeared to be empty. All I could see, looking through the grimy commercial windows that spanned the width of the laundry, was a row of oversized washers on the right and industrial-sized dryers on the left. The interior walls were covered with peeling pink paint, and the brown linoleum floor was scratched but lint free.

Upon entering, I discovered a pixie woman sitting behind a battered, makeshift desk. The pointed tops of her tiny ears poked up from her short white hair—hair that was soft and glowing like a halo.

Her reading and writing surface was an old piece of plywood spanning two battered metal file cabinets. The plywood was partially covered with a blue-flowered plastic cloth. The old woman was reading a newspaper, yellowed with age, that was spread out across the surface.

She smiled kindly at me, her face a cascade of wrinkles rising and falling together in her withered face. I noticed that she had no teeth.

Encouraged, I walked up to her and showed her a photo of Rosie.

"Hi, I'm Emily Menotti. You don't by any chance remember seeing a woman who looks like this?" I asked. "I thought I saw her leaving here last night around seven thirty."

The old woman lifted up a gnarled, arthritic hand and took the photo from me. She studied it for five long seconds.

"I don't know her name," she whispered in a hoarse voice, "but I remember her face. The last time she was here she left without taking her laundry. I've got it in a closet in the back. I've been waiting for her to return for it."

"How long ago was that?"

"Maybe five years."

"Really? And you still remember what she looked like?"

"She was always kind to me," the woman replied. "In the summer she'd bring me a handful of fresh flowers in an empty mayonnaise jar and, in the winter, a cup of hot chocolate from Dunkin' Donuts. I've missed her."

That sounded like the sort of thing Rosie might do—along with forgetting her laundry.

"But," I continued, "I thought I saw her last night, walking out the back door, carrying a basket of clothes."

"Who knows who you saw," she said with a spooky glint in her green eyes.

"And you kept her laundry all this time without throwing it away?"

"I was sure someone would come for it eventually. Let me get it for you."

She eased herself out of a metal folding chair and hobbled to the back room. She returned in no time, pulling a black plastic trash bag behind her. It was obviously too heavy for her to carry, and I hurried up to her and picked it up. It was only half full and not too much for me to manage.

"Please take this and care for it," she said, as if she'd entrusted me with a precious antique. "I'm sure you'll know what to do with it."

"Thank you. I'll come back and let you know what I do with the clothes."

"No need to, honey. I'm sure whatever happens is meant to be."

I left her reluctantly, feeling as if I were breaking a spell to leave this magical laundry inhabited by souls from the past. But Bud was waiting, and I was anxious to get the laundry bag home and examine whatever clues were awaiting me.

Chapter Five

When Bud and I got home, we put away the groceries first and then fixed ourselves cold roast beef sandwiches. We carried our lunch out to the deck along with a bag of chips and two glasses of cold white wine. Bud put Motown on the stereo.

It was just warm enough to sit outside if you wore a sweater, and so we spoke little and enjoyed the ambiance of the woods, the newly green grass, and the soft blue sky. My little rental home backed up to woods that turned from white and yellow in the spring, to green in summer, and finally red and gold in the fall—a kaleidoscope view, compliments of Mother Nature.

When we were done, I carried the bag of clothes out to the deck with us and pulled out Rosie's laundry.

I found the usual lady undergarments, some fresh and lacy, others worn and soft with tiny tears at the seams. There were pastel summer tops, Bermuda shorts, and a few pairs of white socks. I didn't see anything remarkable.

I examined the panties for signs of violence, but there were none. Then I checked the bras for jagged rips or tears and found nothing there either.

Next, I picked up her cotton tops and noticed a lavender one with odd dark marks on the lower front that seemed to line up horizontally about an inch and a half apart. It looked as if she'd held something against her stomach that had left two small, identical marks. The fabric was slightly torn also, like something had been caught there. The marks looked like grease, but it was hard to tell because the clothes had been washed.

I showed the top to Bud. "What do you think these marks are?"

He took the shirt and examined it. "Maybe a makeup applicator?" he offered.

I couldn't really picture a mascara wand or eyeliner pencil that would have two prongs, but I didn't know what else to think.

"Sleep on it," Bud suggested. "Maybe something will come to you."

CHAPTER SIX: MONDAY

After a relaxing weekend, I was back at work as a bank customer service trainer. Metrobank NH Inc. was housed in a rented office building in an industrial park just two miles south of Swansea. The exterior was an unremarkable tan stone with burgundy wood trim. There were few windows, but a broad portico shielded the heavy glass entrance doors from the rain and snow. A uniformed security guard stood behind an enclosure that resembled a ticket window and examined each photo badge, buzzing in the employees or escorting visitors aside to be logged in later.

The guard was usually the same one every morning, a slim African American gentleman named Glenn. He had short curly hair with dew-drop touches of silver. He always smiled and wished you a good day. Over the years I had learned that he was an amateur artist, and I felt honored when, one day, he presented me with a small sketch of myself.

The training room was a windowless white box maybe ten feet by thirty feet with a white board along one wall. Multiple folding tables were lined up end to end to create three rows, each row holding six computers. Wires and cables ran everywhere, and with six monitors and six keyboards per row, there was precious little space for notebooks and pens. An uncomfortable metal folding chair faced each PC.

A large wood and steel desk for the trainer squatted at the front of the room, supporting a PC and a device that projected the information on the trainer's PC onto the wall for all to view. The room was further crowded with two five-foot-tall easels with giant pads of paper. Usually one pad was prefilled with bulleted instructions for the trainees. The other easel held a blank pad for jotting down responses during review exercises.

This was my world eight hours a day. Although I had a personal desk in the call center area, I used that desk mostly to check my e-mail in the morning and retrieve phone messages on my breaks. I loved being hidden away from the call center population and the prying eyes of management. My class and I could joke and laugh without disturbing the rest of the floor. The training room was my kingdom and my refuge.

Today was the first day of a new-hire class for the customer service department of our Metro Credit Card. I loved the first day of a new class. Fifteen fresh faces with a variety of life experiences and skills that I'd build on to make them into successful customer service representatives — or at least some of them, anyway.

I usually started each new class with, what we trainers call, an "ice breaker": a game or quiz that involves revealing not only the participant's name and background but also a few personal tidbits that would help the class get to know each other and feel connected. This morning's group varied in age from twenty- to fifty-somethings. They came from multiple cultural backgrounds, and sorted out roughly 75 percent women to 25 percent men.

After I introduced myself and gave them the basics like class schedule and restroom location, I handed out large index cards. I instructed them to write down three facts about themselves, one of which was true and two were false. Each participant would then read his or hers aloud, and the rest of the class would try to pick the true fact from the false ones.

The game usually went like this: A participant would say "Hi, I'm Jane Smith. I love to cook, I own five cats, and I once had a walk-on part in a Hollywood movie." Next, the others would guess which statement was the true fact. In this case, Jane hated to cook, owned a dog, but had actually been in a Hollywood movie. This revelation might add just a touch of glamour and respect to our perception of her.

For this class, the game did not go so well. The first twelve participants were easy enough — we learned that Elaine owned a horse and had a dozen blue ribbons from riding competitions, Martin had camped for a week in the Grand Canyon, and Josie had once worked as an airline stewardess.

Then we came to Evan, a young man whose true fact was that his father had beaten him when he was a child. I said, "I'm so sorry, Evan," and then we moved on to the young girl who sat beside him.

Her name was Grace. She was a tiny girl, maybe twenty-one or twenty-two years old, with honey-hued curls that draped beautifully around her young face. She was the sort of girl I could imagine on the arm of a burly football player, or some other athletic type, who would create the illusion of his being the protector of this beautiful girl-child, should the need arise.

Her facts were "I was raised by wolves in the Australian outback, I was bitten by a dog as a child, and I was molested by my uncle when I was five." No one said a word. Then she blurted out, "My true fact is that my uncle raped me."

I thought about stopping the game right then when the last trainee spoke up quickly and introduced herself as Martha Allingham. She was a fiftyish woman with short brown hair fading to gray and sparkling blue eyes.

"Hi," she said, "I have eight red-headed children, my home is actually a tree house, and I'm an artist who creates unique sculptures using other folks' discarded treasures."

Grace forgot herself for a moment and clapped her hands in delight just like a child. "I hope they're all true," she said. "It would be so much fun to live in a tree house."

"Well, I don't really live in a tree house," Martha explained, "and I only have two children, who have brown hair, but I am an artist."

Before I could comment, she smiled at Grace and gave her a hug. "Let's have lunch later together in the cafeteria."

"Oh, yes, I'd love that," Grace responded. I smiled inwardly with great relief and outwardly at Martha to thank her for saving the morning.

Chapter Seven

At lunchtime, I went to my cubicle to check my e-mail and was relieved to find only two boring e-mails from upper management about promotions in Boston and volunteers being honored in Portland. I grabbed my lunch bag and headed for the cafeteria.

I found Grace and Martha alone at a corner table. They made a cute tableau—the pretty, young girl excitedly confiding in the still beautiful, older artist.

When I sat down, Grace turned and addressed me.

"I'm awfully sorry for sharing something that was really too personal for the classroom," she said. "It's just that, when I heard what Evan said, I somehow felt compelled to tell my secret also."

"It's okay," I assured her. "People have short memories. They'll forget about it by tomorrow."

I felt the need to add, "Have you ever spoken to another family member or a counselor about what your uncle did? I imagine it's been a hard experience to overcome."

"I did tell my mom, but she said I was imagining things. I'd pretty much forgotten about it until Evan mentioned his experience. I thought I'd put it behind me."

"Well, I know someone who does counseling who would be glad to talk to you about it. I could give you her phone number."

"That's okay. I have my boys. That's all I care about right now." She then gave Martha a knowing smile that told me they'd already discussed it. I hoped the older woman had been of some help.

"You seem so young," I said to Grace, "Are you just out of school?"

"Oh, no. I've been out for a while. I have twin boys who are just three years old. Since their father left, I've really had to struggle to support them. I came to Metrobank to get the benefits like health insurance and day care."

I nodded. Metrobank was one of a small number of employers who provided on-site day care at reduced prices. With two little ones, I could see where that benefit would be huge. "Do you have a picture of them?"

Grace pulled out a photo from her wallet. It showed two gorgeous little boys with similar blonde curls.

"They are the cutest kids. I'll bet they're a handful. What are their names?"

"Oh, they *are* trouble," she said, grinning with pride. "But I'm enjoying every minute of it. Their names are Tyler and Jason. Speaking of them...I think I'll run over to the day-care center and visit for a few minutes before class resumes."

She jumped up, grabbed her tray, and headed for the door. "See you in class," she called back to us.

With that, she left. I sighed, a sigh full of worry. She was so young to have so much responsibility. I hoped she had a mom, a sister, or a friend to help. She would need it.

"How about you?" I asked Martha, opening my container of yogurt then pulling the tab on my can of juice. "Is this a career change for you?"

"Actually, I used to work for Metrobank. I quit a few years ago. I've had two or three less lucrative jobs since. I asked Metrobank what the deal would be if I returned, and they offered to take me back and let me keep all the time I'd previously earned for vacation and sick days."

I noticed she had just finished a sandwich and was starting on a yogurt also. Like me, she tried to eat cheap and healthy. "Why did you quit in the first place? Looking for a better salary?"

"No, I wanted to sell real estate, something I thought I could do part-time while I pursued my artwork. So I left Metro and took the necessary classes to be a realtor, but my real estate career never took off. I couldn't sell space heaters in Alaska. So I've come back to banking."

"I think it'd be fun to visit other homes and see how they're laid out and decorated. I'd probably love a job like that."

"Well, I agree with you about going into houses, but you have to be able to sell, and by that, I mean you have to be able to push. I just couldn't do it."

"Well, I'm glad I talked to you then. What about the financial end of that? I've heard it's all on commission. Did your husband support you while you sold real estate?"

"No, he had jettisoned me long before...for a younger woman. On my thirtieth birthday to be exact. I've made peace with it."

"Then how did you survive?"

"I had a second part-time job. I usually did retail or day care. I'll never forget my first part-time job selling cosmetics at Lacy's Department Store. My friend Rosie got me that job. But as you can see, I don't wear cosmetics and I was a total failure there too."

"Are you talking about Rose Hamlin?"

"Yes, did you know her? She died about five years ago."

"I did! She never mentioned you, I don't think."

"Well, we weren't close friends at that point. I knew her from high school, and I'd see her off and on at the mall or at a restaurant and we'd talk. I was shocked to hear she died of a heart attack. She always looked so healthy."

"That's what I said! I knew her pretty well at that time. I was the one who found her body and called 9-1-1. I'm so glad to meet you!"

"I'm glad to meet you too. How awful for you that you found her body. Had Rosie calmed down any in middle age? She was always bouncing from one friend to another."

"No change, I'm afraid. She had a volatile personality."

Martha smiled. "Well, I'm sorry to cut you short, but I have a few personal calls to make before I come back to class. Will you excuse me?"

"Of course. See you in class."

I watched Martha carry her trash to the bin and disappear through the double doors to the employee lounge. I couldn't wait to ask her more questions about Rosie.

The afternoon was uneventful as we reviewed the employee code of conduct, dress regulations, and the various help lines for health issues, child care, and elder care. I let them go a little early and saw Grace rush out the door, anxious to rescue her boys from day care. Martha seemed in a hurry to go also.

In my job at Metrobank, I got to know all the employees at our site. Besides training new hires and holding mini-meetings in the workstation pods for updates and quick changes, I conducted training sessions for company-wide reminders on information security and our clean-desk policy.

I was also a security officer, which meant I did random checks of employees' desks to make sure that drawers were locked in the evenings and no papers with account holder information — such as name, address, phone or social security number — were left lying out.

I also did quality reviews of the reps' telephone conversations.

That evening, after I'd reviewed my lesson plan for the next day, I sat at my desk and dialed into the telephone monitoring system. I listened to a few good calls, where the reps were helpful and courteous, and filled out the corresponding Quality Customer Service Review sheets that would go to their supervisors. Then I listened to a call belonging to my least favorite representative, Claire Hunter. I could tell she was talking with her mouth full, and I noted that she greeted the customer with a surly, "Yeah?"

The caller was a woman who wanted to report that she was going to be late on that month's payment. "And what exactly did you want me to do about that?" was Claire's helpful response.

"I was hoping you might waive the late fee," the woman said. "My husband lost his job and we won't have any money until his unemployment kicks in."

What Claire told her next, though accurate, was not nicely stated. "There's nothing I can do until the payment is actually late. I've got other callers on hold. I'll have to disconnect now. Call back when your bill is past due." With that, the line went dead.

Claire was one of the bank's most challenging employees. She ate greasy fried chicken at her desk and then left the bones and dirty napkins lying about when she went home in evening. She called in sick constantly and, at least four times a year, had a relative or close friend die, which required compassionate leave. She was rude to the customers and often confused the credit policies and procedures she was supposed to explain.

One day I saw her put a customer on hold, move to the empty desk next to her, pick up the phone there, and call her mother. They talked for maybe five minutes, then she put her mother on hold, went back to her first call, and quickly terminated that conversation so she could get back to her mother. You couldn't ask for a worse example of a customer service representative.

I often wondered why she was never fired until, one day, she chatted me up in the cafeteria. She bragged about her big house and her expensive car, both of which she had bought with money from successful lawsuits against various car manufacturers and insurance companies. She said she knew her rights and had a lawyer on retainer who could file a lawsuit with only twenty-four hours' notice. I quickly figured out that the bank was scared of her.

After listening to her phone call and filling out her Quality Customer Service Review form with low marks and lots of comments, I decided to listen to one last call.

I pressed the "Next" button, and a little-girl voice said, "Hi, Emily. I need you," and then there was silence. It was Rosie's voice. It had been recorded in the last twenty-four hours. Who would play such a prank on me? Or was it a prank?

Chapter Eight

I drove home feeling troubled and depressed. After surviving Casey's greeting and putting on jeans and a tee, I took the glass of wine Bud handed me and sat down next to him on the sofa.

At the end of a long day, it was heaven to sink down into the blue-flowered cushions of my country cottage sofa and rest my feet on the braided rug that formed a large oval on the hardwood floor. I've never cared much for formal living and dining rooms. I don't see the point of living rooms that people never live in and dining rooms where people rarely eat.

At dinnertime, Bud and I set our plates and glasses on the coffee table and ate our dinner while watching *Jeopardy* and *Family Feud*. Soft, ivory curtains stirred at the windows and Casey's sleeping form at my feet completed my picture of domestic bliss.

Relaxed at last, I told Bud about the voice on the phone.

"Who do you think it was?" I asked him. "It really spooked me."

"One of the other customer service reps trying to get ahold of you, that's all."

"But it was Rosie's voice."

"Couldn't have been, plain and simple. You were mistaken."

Bud was odd to my way of thinking, but not unlike other men I'd dated. They refused to acknowledge anything that didn't fit into their frame of reference. Voices from beyond the grave—hogwash! It just couldn't be, and he was going to ignore all evidence to the contrary.

The other weird thing about Bud was that he was a creationist, something that completely surprised me when we began arguing about evolution one night. He was a former policeman, a detective, a believer in hard facts and evidence, and yet, when I told him that science had absolutely proven the theory of evolution, he chose to ignore it.

"There's no reason it couldn't have happened the way it is in the Bible," he said. "God is all-powerful. He can arrange things any way He wants." This from a man who didn't even go to church.

"You've got to help me here, hon. Even if you don't believe I heard Rosie's voice, how would I go about investigating her death? How could I find out if there was anything the coroner missed? Did they take photos of her body from all angles during the autopsy?"

"Well, yes, they should have. They would be on file. You want to see some of those?"

"Yes, it's a starting place. Do you know anyone who could get those for me?"

"Not hard copies but, maybe, online photos. My friend Mitch works in the coroner's office. Let me talk to him."

Later that evening I got a phone call from my friend Melinda, another acquaintance I'd made when searching for Darcie. Melinda claimed that she had psychic abilities, and although I doubted her somewhat — because, in her shoes, I would have been playing Powerball regularly — I had to admit she'd been right about Darcie.

She was taller than I, maybe five feet ten, and fifteen years younger. She had shoulder-length straight hair that was currently blonde and a soft, olive complexion with large hazel eyes. She'd be been blessed with a perfectly proportioned face, and with no makeup, one quickly noticed the intelligence in her eyes and the kindness in her voice. Why Melinda didn't have a steady boyfriend was beyond me.

"How ya doing?" she asked.

"I'm doing good. What have you been up to?"

"You should have heard the *Howard Stern Show* today; he was so funny!"

"You know, I work. Unlike you...the domestic goddess."

Melinda was actually a trust-fund baby and worked only sporadically when she got bored.

"You need to get satellite radio. Then you could listen any time."

"When? Bud would never listen. The topics, not to mention the language, would certainly offend him."

"Oh well, so what have you been up to?"

I told her how I saw Rosie exiting the Laundromat and heard her voice on the phone. To explain why that was strange, I then told her about Rosie's death and how suspicious I was of her having a heart attack.

"I knew something was up with you," she said. "That's why I called. Let me do my own investigation. I'll give myself a suggestion when I go to sleep tonight, and maybe I'll dream something that gives us a clue."

"Bud doesn't believe that I saw and heard Rosie. He thinks I'm misinterpreting events. The person I saw at the Laundromat was just someone who happened to look like Rosie and got into a waiting car; the voice was a customer service rep calling."

"Well, you know I'm not going to tell you that. I'll call you again tomorrow. Nighty night, lady."

"You too."

Chapter Nine: Tuesday

Bud was true to his word, and the next day when I returned from work, he said, "Check your e-mail. I sent you some photos."

Then he handed me a glass of wine. "You'll need this. They're pretty gruesome."

Going to the computer, I opened the e-mail Bud sent me. There were a dozen photo attachments. I closed my eyes for a second and thought about what I might see. Gathering my courage, I opened my eyes and clicked on the first photo.

It was horrible. The shot was an overhead photo showing Rosie's naked body after the autopsy had been performed. There was the classic, roughly sewn Y shape starting from each shoulder and coming to meet at a point just below her breasts, and then continuing in one line down to her groin. She looked like a poorly sewn rag doll.

Her face and skin were mottled, her eyes were wide and bulging, and her hair was a greasy mess. This was nothing like the waxen mannequins on TV crime shows. I couldn't drink the wine. I felt like I was going to be sick. This had been my dear friend. I didn't want to remember her this way.

I moved on. The other photos were pictures of arms, legs, her head from three sides, upper torso front and back, and lower torso front and back. These were less upsetting because the body parts were photographed without the face in the photo frame.

The lower front torso shot was the worst in terms of my feeling that her personhood had been violated, although in truth, the photo was probably business as usual. I just wasn't used to seeing clinical photos of a feminine groin. I wondered if she shaved that area regularly or if standard autopsy procedure was to shave it.

I saw no obvious injuries anywhere.

For my purposes I was primarily concerned with her head and upper torso, thinking foul play would most likely have occurred in these areas. I didn't relish magnifying the view to 200 percent.

In the photos of the back of her head, there was nothing identifiable as a wound. On her upper torso, there were a few light bruises that could have occurred when she fell.

On her lower front torso there were a few abrasions that looked like scratched pimples or angry mosquito bites. They seemed to roughly line up with the marks I'd seen on her lavender top. I wondered about those, but they didn't look like needle injection sites or anything else especially lethal.

In an accompanying e-mail, Bud explained that, after calling on his acquaintances at the coroner's office, he had also been able to learn that the tox report found no drugs or other abnormalities. So I was still at a loss for a reasonable cause of death.

As I sat at the computer trying to puzzle out this mystery, Bud came up behind me and started massaging my neck and shoulders.

"Pretty bad, huh?" he asked.

"I'll say. But look at these two dark dots here on Rosie's stomach. They match up with the two marks on her lavender top. Any idea what they are?"

"Could be just bruises or small cuts," he said and looked away. He didn't seem too interested.

"What's your professional opinion?" I asked.

"I always operate under the philosophy that the simplest explanation is probably the truest. Isn't that Occam's razor?"

"Ah, I think I see some education other than the police academy shining through. Did you go to college?"

"Just two years at Keene. Always meant to go back and get a four-year degree. Never got around to it."

"And you studied philosophy?" I was amazed. This from a creationist? There was no pigeonholing Bud.

"You get electives, even in a two-year program." He sounded slightly offended, as if I had doubted his intelligence. "Now, come on out to the deck and keep me company. Let a little wine wash those images out of your mind."

"Will do. And thanks for getting these photos. I don't know if they'll help me any, but I had to look."

"Understood. You'd have made a good detective."

I took that as high praise indeed.

Chapter Ten: Wednesday

The next day was a workday and business as usual. Grace was in class bright and early, but I was dismayed to learn that Evan had not returned. Perhaps he'd been offered a better job elsewhere.

Martha had taken Evan's seat next to Grace. I hoped she would be a good influence.

My training class had received their sign-on IDs and temporary passwords. We spent the day practicing logging in and out of all the systems they would need, which were actually quite a few since they needed to access customers' credit card account information and the bank's payment processing software; log into a separate system for e-mail; and, last but not least, navigate the Human Resources website for recording their hours each week and managing payroll deductions. The rest of week they would be accessing dummy accounts to see how charges were recorded and minimum payments calculated.

On Thursday, they also learned how to change address and telephone information, and by the week's end, they were removing late fees and role-playing customer calls with each other. I was pretty happy with most of them, but Grace was struggling.

In my time as a trainer I've seen lots of different types of workers from the super-organized types, who arrive ten minutes early and keep copious notes, to the social butterflies, who arrive late and want to spend half the class conversing with their neighbor. Contrary to what you might think, neither type is an easy prediction of success or failure.

Social butterflies might have trouble remembering a particular procedure, but their skill at keeping the customer flattered and happy outweighs their scrambling for the right screen and forgetting their passwords every other day. Super-organized employees might be impatient with ditzy callers who have forgotten their due date or need help understanding their statement.

Poor Grace was neither of these. She couldn't find her class password when logging in each morning, she couldn't remember which screen the interest rate was on or how to remove a late fee, and she was short and terse with pretend callers during role-playing exercises.

Then she would come up to me after class and ask, "Was I alright?"

I'd give her a few pointers and suggest she study her notes in the evening. "Oh, I can't do that," she'd say. "The boys keep me too busy with dinner and baths. By bedtime I'm exhausted, and I'm asleep five minutes after they are."

What could I do?

Friday night, after a week of little success with Grace, I arrived home tired and discouraged. What do you do with an employee like Grace who so badly needed both the paycheck and the benefits? Then I thought of Claire Hunter and decided what the hell. If the bank could keep Claire, they could also keep Grace.

That evening, as Bud and I enjoyed our drinks and usual Friday night treat of sausage and onion pizza, the phone rang. It was Melinda.

"Can I come over?"

"Of course! Have a glass of wine with us."

She was there in twenty minutes. Casey greeted her warmly, tail wagging in welcome.

"Pizza?" I asked as I poured her a drink.

"No thanks. I wanted to tell you that I've been having some bizarre dreams this week. I've never met your friend Rosie, but the woman in my dreams is always wearing red clothes, so I thought of red roses and figured that's who it is."

"And what have you been dreaming?"

"I keep seeing car accidents and police cars. The woman in my dream is sitting in her car and there are wrecked cars all around her. Policemen arrive and are surrounding her car, and they look like they're threatening her. Then I wake up."

"That's odd. I don't recall Rosie having a car accident right before she died. But she was always getting traffic tickets."

"Remember, dreams aren't to be taken literally. The policemen could just be authority figures. The car accidents could represent chaos in her personal life. What did she do for a living?"

"She was the manager of the cosmetics department at Lacy's. The only authority figures would be store managers. Unless we're talking authority figures in her personal life, but she wasn't dating anybody that I knew of. I was one of her few friends, and I'm certainly no authority figure."

"Were there unhappy customers who'd complained about her?"

"Well, yes. She could get quite defensive when a woman claimed her makeup hadn't made her look as attractive as the salesperson said it would. But I don't quite see these women as being portrayed as police officers in your dreams."

"It's hard to know. But if you just go on the emotional feel of the dreams, she was angry *and* terrified."

"Poor Rosie. I can't remember her saying anything about being frightened."

A sudden knock on the door interrupted my thoughts. Casey instantly got up and started barking. Bud and I looked at each other. People rarely showed up unannounced. I excused myself and went to answer it.

As if in response to our conversation, I opened the front door to see a somber-faced policewoman, very tall, maybe six feet one or two. She had her dark hair pulled back in a ponytail so that all you really noticed was a large, pale face and dark eyes. She wore a frown with her dark blue uniform; the effect was quite intimidating. Casey had stopped barking, which was usually a signal that he recognized the caller.

"I'm Tanya," she said in a voice loud enough to carry through the house. "Bud's daughter."

Chapter Eleven

"I'm Emily," I managed to squeak out. I was really caught off guard. Bud had said he had a daughter whom he didn't see very often — saying something about she never forgave him for divorcing her mother. However, this was not the pretty, rebellious young girl I'd pictured.

"Please come in," I added, and motioned her toward the living room.

She strode in, boots clicking on the hardwood floor. Bud had obviously heard her voice and was on his feet to meet her. They didn't shake hands or hug or show any signs of affection.

"Hi, Dad," was all she said, staring at him with that frown still on her face. No doubt she disapproved of me, or my home, or maybe the whole world for all I knew.

Bud was not a man easily upset or at a loss for words, but it seemed to take him a few seconds to get his bearings — a first in my relationship with him.

Finally, he broke the silence by saying, "Hi, Baby. How are you? This is my girlfriend, Emily, and her friend, Melinda. Girls, this is my daughter, Tanya."

Tanya turned and nodded at me and stayed standing in the hallway. She ignored Melinda completely. I glanced at Melinda and noticed that she was looking at Tanya oddly, like there was something else going on other than a friendly introduction.

"I need to speak to you, Dad." Tanya said. "I've been having a problem. I want to run it by you."

"Please, sit down," I said and motioned to the empty seat next to Bud on the sofa. "Would you like a glass of wine or a soda?"

"I don't drink alcohol," she said with a hard look at Bud. "Coke or Pepsi is fine."

I hurried to the kitchen to obey what almost sounded like a command. The chill she'd brought into the room had spooked me and I couldn't wait to leave.

When I returned with her Coke and more wine for Melinda and me, I saw that she was sitting stiffly on the sofa, talking to her father. She looked at me briefly, her eyes dismissing me like a servant as she accepted her glass of soda, and then continued her conversation.

"I don't understand it," I heard her say. "It doesn't make any sense. If I wasn't evaluated twice a year by the staff shrink, I'd almost think I was going crazy."

As I topped off Melinda's glass of wine, she gave me a raised-eyebrow look that said something important was happening and she couldn't wait to talk to me about it.

I noticed Bud had put his martini on a side table and seemed to be ignoring it—a most unusual move for him.

I looked again at Tanya.

"When you were under stress at work, did you ever find strange things happening to you around your house? I seem to be misplacing things, even though I know exactly where I left them."

Bud looked at her quizzically.

"I have a key holder with hooks by my front door. I always put my keys on a hook when I walk in the door. I make a conscious effort now to remember that I put them there. And yet when I go back to get them, they're gone."

"Do you always find them again?" Bud asked.

"Yes, but in such odd places, like the bathroom countertop or in the refrigerator or, one time, stuffed in a pair of old sneakers. There's no way I would do that. My husband assures me it's not him playing a joke, and he doesn't see me put my keys in these odd places. In fact, he swears he's seen me put my keys on the hook, but then when I'm ready to leave, they're not there."

Bud didn't comment when she paused, so she kept talking.

"It's been a nightmare. I have to get ready to leave for work fifteen minutes earlier than usual now because I know I'll have to spend that much time looking for my keys."

"Is it just the keys, or are you losing other objects as well?"

"Other things, but mostly my keys."

"Could you be sleepwalking?"

"Rick says no, though he can't be positive. He's a pretty light sleeper, and he thinks he'd know if I were getting out of bed in the middle of the night."

"You must be sleepwalking and moving your keys or else Rick is trying to make you think you're crazy. How has your relationship been lately?"

"Okay. But he wants children. I just can't get interested in the idea of being a parent. Other than that, we're pretty agreeable. But you never had anything like that happen to you while you were on the force?"

"No, nothing like that. When I was stressed I usually went down to the bar and drowned my sorrows with the other cops. Law enforcement is not an easy life. Your buddies are really the only ones who understand."

"But I don't even have that, Dad. Besides not liking to drink, there's only one other woman on the force, and we work opposite shifts. I can't see me hanging out at the bar with the guys, drinking Coke while they drink beer and complain about their wives and children."

"I can see that. But I think you need to relax, hon. This will straighten itself out eventually. Maybe you should try yoga...or meditation...or going to church."

Tanya seemed offended by these suggestions.

"You'd never do any of those things," she said accusingly.

"Well, maybe not, but they're the only solutions I've got."

Tanya stood. She was even more intimidating if you were sitting down. She seemed ten feet tall, like a dark blue giant. As she headed for the door, the Taser and handcuffs attached to her wide leather belt jangled as she moved. Her presence somehow made me feel like a convict.

"It was nice to meet you," she said and looked at me briefly. Again, she totally ignored Melinda.

"So glad to meet you too," I said hoarsely.

"Let me know what happens," Bud called out to her as she left. "I want to know either way."

I followed her to the door.

"Come back anytime," I told her. "We'd love to see you again."

"Oh, I will," she said and strode away. I shivered, glad to see her go.

When I turned away from the door, Melinda was on her feet and heading out also. I wanted to talk to her, but she seemed in a hurry.

"I have an appointment at ten," she explained. The SRBPS has an investigation tonight and I promised I'd join them."

I nodded. SRBPS was short for the Severn River Basin Paranormal Society.

"Where?" I asked.

"The Old Stone Mill," she said, mentioning a renovated property on the Severn River that had been converted into expensive condos. "The residents are complaining of odd noises and apparitions."

"Could I come?" I asked. I knew it would mean losing a night's sleep, but I didn't care. I explained, "Rosie lived there for a while with a boyfriend, Derek something, back when I first met her." I smiled, "Maybe she's causing trouble...that's not unlike her."

"Great! Are you sure you're up for it? Might be a long night. Come to think of it, your knowing one of the former residents might be helpful."

I looked at Bud. I knew he didn't approve, but he'd just have to suck it up.

"I doubt I can stop you," he said, shaking his head in disapproval.

"We'll talk in the morning. Just let me grab a jacket, Melinda, and I'm good to go."

I got my windbreaker and gave Bud a quick kiss good-bye.

"Be careful," he warned.

"Don't worry."

I jumped into Melinda's black SUV, looking forward to the adventure.

Chapter Twelve

"I'm glad you're coming," Melinda said as she started her car. "I wanted to tell you what I saw tonight."

"What did you see?"

"When Tanya walked in, she had an intense aura around her that was unusual. It was mostly a bright lemon yellow, which indicates fear. She's very frightened or worried about something. But I also saw flares of emerald green and, sometimes, a wave of black."

"She doesn't look like she'd be afraid of anything," I offered. "She certainly intimidated me."

"That's her self-defense mechanism. You know, like in football. They always say the best defense is a good offense."

"I get you. What does the emerald green signify?"

"What green usually means, jealousy and resentment. Without knowing her better, I couldn't tell you why."

"And the black, that sounds pretty scary all by itself."

"No, not scary. Sad, actually. Black means grief, and if it's in your aura, it means you haven't dealt with it yet. It's still bottled up inside you, causing havoc with your body and soul."

"I almost feel sorry for her."

"Me too."

We rode without speaking for a while. Melinda had a beautiful Maura O'Connell CD playing. Her softly crooning voice sang of love and grief, and one song even made me smile because it was so honest. It was about losing her temper and wanting to take back the stinging words she'd said in anger to her partner. I could imagine myself singing those same words to my ex-husband, but it was way too late now. I guess it touched my own treasure trove of love and grief.

We finally arrived at the Old Stone Mill Luxury Condominiums. The entry roundabout was filled with minivans and SUVs, all black, all with doors open and wires running every which way between the vehicles and the building.

Melinda filled me in on the building's history. The structure had once been a cotton mill where some one hundred looms had put out up to ten miles of cotton fabric per day.

The mill had opened in the early nineteenth century when raw cotton was plentiful and shipped up from the South to the mills in the North for processing. At one time, the mill had employed about 350 people, many of them French Canadians who had come for the jobs and later settled in the area. The looms ran day and night, and were rumored to have employed children as young as ten years old.

The Civil War had halted production temporarily, and after the war, the shipments began again but never in the same volume. Over time, cotton weaving shifted to factories built in the South. When the Great Depression came, it silenced the industry completely.

The property had been abandoned until the 1980s; then a Swansea businessman had come up with the idea of turning the site into condominiums. The stone building was gutted from within and rebuilt as twelve luxury units with Jacuzzi tubs and SubZero appliances.

The waterwheel of the mill itself still turned with the force of the dank river water and could be seen through a glass wall that replaced one wall of the first-floor common area. The common area boasted a fieldstone fireplace, a small kitchen, and a few restrooms and was used for residents' meetings and socializing.

The night presented an eerie scene, with the tall trees looming against the starless sky, the mill wheel creaking with the weight of the river, and the darkened structure of condos crouched in silence. The windows looked back at us, black and empty, with no light anywhere except for the small pinpricks of red to tell us that the ghost-hunting equipment was up and running.

Renovations appeared to be ongoing: one whole outside wall of the residence was covered from top to bottom with industrial-weight plastic to keep out the weather. The sound of the river, spilling water over the rocks just fifty yards away, infused the night and the scene with a brooding melancholy.

It is well-known in investigative circles that renovations often result in paranormal activity. Water is also known to attract spirits.

Since this had been a cotton mill where workers may have died in industrial accidents, their spirits could still be here, maybe not even aware that they had died. As fantastic as that sounds, electronic voice phenomena, or EVP, support such claims.

A large man, dressed in black jeans and hoodie and holding a mini-flashlight, directed Melinda to park her vehicle in the back of the parking lot. In her headlights we could see the residents huddled around a picnic table drinking mugs of something and eating sandwiches. No one other than the investigators could be in the building while the SRBPS technicians were working.

Melinda introduced me to Ed, one of the crew, and explained that I knew someone who had lived there and had since passed on. She suggested I might be helpful in recognizing a voice on an EVP monitor. Did he know if a guy named Derek still lived there?

"Most of the residents are over by the picnic table. Why don't you go over and ask them?"

So we walked toward the picnic table and found a crowd of mostly twenty-somethings in workout clothes and sneakers. A few older couples huddled together, and one lone figure tried to look as if he didn't know any of the people.

Then among the huddled residents I saw my trainee, Martha Allingham.

"Martha! Do you live here?" I called out.

She separated herself from the crowd and walked over to where Melinda and I stood.

"Hi, teach," she said. "I didn't recognize you with your rain hood pulled over your face. What are you doing here?"

"I'm a friend of one of the investigators. Martha, this is Melinda... and Melinda, Martha." I turned to Melinda and explained, "Martha's in my latest training class at Metrobank."

"Seen any ghosts?" Melinda asked, half-jokingly.

"Well, not me, but I'm the one who called the SRBPS. Since I've moved in here a few weeks ago, my boyfriend has been having problems with things moving on their own and seeing apparitions. I've never seen the apparitions, only Derek has."

At the mention of his name, the man who'd had his back turned to us spun around. "I'm Derek," he announced. "What about me?"

I recognized him immediately. I'd only met him a few times when I came by to pick up Rosie for an evening out, but he was an unforgettable man. He was blonde, he was tan, he was six feet tall with just the right amount of muscle definition. His cigarette dangled from the right corner of his mouth.

In anybody's book he was gorgeously handsome with just the right amount of bad-boy charisma. When he smiled and focused his dark-lashed green eyes on you, your heart stopped.

Or at least it did in the first few seconds. Then he opened his mouth to speak and your opinion rapidly reformed itself.

"Hey, doll-face," he said, suddenly recognizing me. "How's it shaking?"

Rosie had always explained that his good looks and bedroom performance were worth any amount of rude behavior. I'd always disagreed.

"How are you, Derek?" I answered.

"Still knockin' 'em dead, Em. Still knockin' 'em dead," he said, tapping the ashes of his cigarette into a soda can. "How's 'bout you?"

"Still slaving away at the bank. What's going on with your condo?"

"Seems we need an investigation. Lots of noise, weird lights, that kinda stuff. It spooks some people. Not me." He took a drag of his cigarette to emphasis his nonchalance. He held it between his thumb and index finger like an old movie thug.

Martha walked over and put an arm around Derek's waist. They exchanged smiles. I felt uncomfortable.

"Looks like they're renovating the north side," I said.

"Well, yeah. Tree fell the last storm," Derek explained.

"No one hurt?"

"Luckily, no. Just knocked down a buncha old siding."

As he spoke, he and Martha moved a step closer. He'd aged little in the past five or six years. There were the usual lines around the eyes and mouth that come with middle age, but he'd aged gracefully and looked just a little more ruggedly handsome than before.

"You know Rosie died," I said to him. "Five years ago."

"Yeah, I heard. Too bad." He dropped the rest of his cigarette and ground out the glow with his boot. "She was a great chick. A little wacky, sometimes, but still a great chick. Couldn't get enough of me."

I let it pass. Martha looked away and made no comment.

"Why'd you two ever break up? Rosie never wanted to talk about it too much. She just kept insisting you were an asshole."

"Me?" He sounded offended. "She was the crazy one. She could never admit she was wrong about anything. She always had to have the last word. It got tiresome. A man can only take so much verbal abuse."

"I'll second that," said a man who appeared out of nowhere and stood next to Martha. He held a mug that smelled like coffee.

"The screaming arguments you two had annoyed the whole building. That woman could carry on for hours. I can't tell you how many nights we almost called the police just to get her to shut up."

"So you never complained?" I asked the man.

"No, we didn't want to get involved, and I didn't want that woman mad at me."

Derek smiled like a trophy winner. He held his fists up and sparred a little into the cool night air.

"She was a fighter, but I always calmed her down eventually. At some point the passion of the moment would overtake her and make her want to have sex. Then I knew it was all over. Sometimes, I do miss the excitement."

Martha gave him an odd look, and he added, "Not that there isn't something to be said for steadier, more committed relationships." Martha frowned, disengaged her arm, and walked away without a response.

I didn't doubt his story about Rosie's temper. I'd had one or two disagreements with Rosie myself. The funny thing about them was that I was never really sure what they were about. We'd be talking and suddenly she'd accuse me of not understanding her. Then she'd bring up other times I hadn't understood her and accuse me of not caring enough about our relationship to try and understand her.

I was always flummoxed and usually dealt with the situation by apologizing and making an excuse to go home. We'd pay our check at the restaurant or leave the mall in stony silence, get in our cars, and go our separate ways. And the next time she called, she always acted as if the argument had never happened.

I could imagine how difficult living with her would have been. Derek had obviously managed it his own way.

"Emily, you ready to go in?" Melinda tugged at my sleeve and suggested I join her and a small crew of investigators as they began their walk through the building.

I was glad to get away from Derek and the bad memories he'd conjured up.

Suddenly a bolt of lightning split the sky and struck the earth just north of the condos. In the brief jolt of light, I saw the old mill shiver with the force of the electricity. The four-story stone building gaped back at me with its empty black windows. Just before the flash ended, I caught a glimpse of a figure in the open front door. One of the ghost hunters? Maybe. But it looked like Rosie to me.

"Equipment's fried," I heard James Willis, one of the founders of SRBPS, yell out. "We're done for the night."

"We'll have to reschedule," his partner Greg Lowe said.

"Damn," said Melinda, but I was again glad.

I was frightened and looked forward to going home to my cozy bed.

As Melinda and I rode back into Swansea, the rain began to pelt down on us and I was glad for the protection of her large SUV. The wind was battering the bushes and trees along the road, and we didn't talk as Melinda wrestled with the steering to keep the car on course. After fifteen minutes the storm seemed to have blown itself out, and the rain let up to a drizzle.

I thought this might be a good time to ask her a question I'd often wondered about.

"Mel, I know you have some psychic gifts. Have you ever thought of using that power for financial gain? I was wondering why you don't play the lottery to see if you can guess the winning numbers."

"It's not about numbers and data, and I can't predict the future. I'm what's called a clairsentient. My so-called psychic abilities have to do with emotions."

"You pick up on what people are feeling?"

"Yes, both people alive and people who are no longer living. Their emotions are like an invisible footprint of where they are and where they've been."

"Cool! But how do you know the emotions are there?"

"Emotions are like gravity. You can't see them or touch them, but you feel them and you see their effects. Sort of like a scientist can look at the universe and explain how it came to exist simply by studying rocks. Like a geologist, I study a person or place and see the residual effects of past or present events and emotions."

"So it's like a level of, I don't know, awareness that not everyone has."

"Yes, like not everyone has the talent to be a neurosurgeon or an opera singer."

"So you can't tell me what numbers to play?" I joked.

"You're not the first person to ask me that. I think some people with second sight try to use it that way, but not most of us. It's been my experience that people like me, who have this gift, are also given a strong moral sense. We want to help people. We want to ease their pain. We want to bring a little more love and peacefulness into their lives. Even if we won the lottery, though, and gave the money away, we'd know that money's not usually the answer to a person's problems."

"I see that. You're right. When I think about the really tough times in my life when I didn't have money, they weren't tough because I didn't have money. They were tough because I made wrong choices, like who I married or what job I took. Sometimes I wasted my money on useless things."

"Stop and think about that, Em. When you made that choice of who to marry, why were you marrying him?"

"I was crazy in love with him."

"So you didn't value money as much as you valued other things, like love?"

"Yes, you're right."

"So you made the right choice at the time."

Leave it to Melinda to make me feel better about what I thought was my big mistake.

"How are things with you and Bud?" she asked.

"Wonderful. This is the happiest I've been in a long time. I'm hoping we can keep this going and maybe get married at some point. Bud has brought it up once or twice, but he's never actually come out and asked me to marry him."

"You know, I grew up here and know most of the people in town. I've heard stories about him and his buddies. They all used to drink a lot, but I've never heard anything else...like his being aggressive or violent. Still, I worry about you sometimes."

"I've heard those stories too, and it's true that I did meet him in a bar. But he seems to know when to stop. I've never seen him drunk. It's in the back of my mind, though. If he did ask me to marry him, I'd want to wait a while just to see if, over time, a problem develops."

"You're not upset with me that I've brought it up?"

"No, I take it as a sign of your friendship. I'd do the same for you."

We were at my house now. I told her thanks, gave her a sideways hug, and jumped out to run up the path in the rain.

"I'll call you," Melinda shouted.

"Okay, thanks for the adventure," I yelled back and yanked open the front door. Melinda sped off into the night.

Bud was waiting up for me.

"I'm glad you're home," he said. "You can't blame me for being worried about you traipsing around an old building late at night, especially with this storm."

"Glad to be home too," I said, hanging my jacket on a dining room chair to dry. "They never started their investigation, however. There was a huge lightning strike close by and it shut down all their equipment."

"No one was hurt?"

"No, thank goodness, but in all the excitement, I forgot to ask Melinda about Rosie. I need an action plan. I need to figure out what happened to her."

"Well, in your shoes, I'd go back to the people who saw her in the last day or two of her life. Didn't you say she worked at Lacy's Department Store?"

"Yeah, she was the manager of the cosmetics department."

"Why don't you talk to her coworkers?"

"Bud, I love you! That's a great idea. Why didn't I think of that?" I gave him a quick hug and a kiss on the cheek.

"I'll do that first thing Saturday," I said.

Chapter Thirteen: Saturday

Lacy's Department Store is the anchor store in a mall on the edge of Swansea's town limits. The mall is on Route 9, the road that winds west from Keene through lower New Hampshire and that, eventually, takes you to Brattleboro and the intersection with I-91, which then takes you farther south to the East Coast's major artery I-95.

It isn't the busiest mall except maybe at Christmas, but it gives employment to quite a few otherwise jobless New Englanders. Things might be booming in Boston and New Haven, but the economic life of Northern New England has been as slow as Vermont maple syrup.

I parked my car within a few yards of Lacy's entrance and wandered in past half-dressed, alien-looking mannequins with fine pale fingers either pointing nowhere or, perhaps, to the unseen mother ship.

Being May and also Memorial Day weekend, the bathing suit sales were in full swing. The aisles were cluttered with racks and racks of tiny tops and bottoms most of us would look laughable wearing — unless, of course, you find puckered white flesh spilling over little swaths of flowered polyester attractive.

The cosmetics department was lit up like a crystal palace. It was so bright it almost hurt my eyes, and I worried for the migraine-prone who might wander by and end up with stabbing pain from the glare of so many bright lights.

As I tried to shield my eyes from the glow of a thousand suns, my olfactory senses were assaulted by the flowery scents of Dior, Calvin, and Chanel all battling for attention. A small girl with a glass atomizer offered me a spritz of the latest creation. I declined, but I did ask her if the department manager was in.

"Nora's behind the Miracale counter," she said and pointed to a blue and yellow draped display with glistening bottles of lotions and potions.

"Thank you," I replied and headed that way.

Like the department she worked in, the thirty-something young woman behind the counter was tastelessly overdone.

"What can I help you with today?" she said, a little too loudly.

"Hi, I'm Emily."

"Well, hi there, Emily, I'm Nora. How are you?"

Nora was a diminutive person, wearing a tiny black spandex tube top that exposed breasts which were too large for her frame and appeared ready to jump out of their nest at any moment.

"I used to buy cosmetics from a woman who worked here and I haven't seen her in a long time." I began. "I was hoping to get her advice on something. I think her name was Rosie."

"Oh my gawd, Rosie! She died years ago!"

"Died? Oh, I'm so sorry to hear that. I really enjoyed talking to her. What happened?"

"Heart attack. Imagine that! Forty-some years old. You just never know, do you?"

"But she looked so healthy!"

"I know. We all said that. But she was upset about something, and maybe her heart wasn't strong enough to handle it."

"I know she used to talk about a boyfriend. Do you think he did something to upset her?"

"That SOB? A black eye, maybe, but not a heart attack. She was a pretty tough cookie when it came to boyfriends."

"Did anything else happen around that time that might have upset her?"

Nora was looking at me a little askance now. I wasn't asking about makeup or perfume. I could see in her dark eyes the question if she should be giving out all this personal information to a stranger. I smiled my most winning smile and picked up a bottle of something to distract her. "I really liked her," I added.

"Well, I remember the day before she died. She came back from lunch and was all upset. She'd had a car accident earlier, just a fender bender really, and she wanted to sue the driver, or maybe the driver threatened to sue her. She called a lawyer and arranged to meet him later. I didn't hear the details, but I gathered it was business. She was very angry. Talked about teaching someone a lesson."

"Poor Rosie, do you think she'd been injured?"

"She didn't look hurt, at least not physically, but if you knew Rosie, you'd know her feelings were very easily disturbed."

"Ah, yes. I can see that. Do you remember the lawyer's name?"

Nora's eyes narrowed, and she shook her vibrant red hair in answer. Perhaps I'd gone too far with my questions. I didn't sound like an occasional shopper sorry to lose her cosmetics coach. But then she relented.

"Something Kennedy? An ambulance-chaser type. Longish brown hair and cheap suit." Just great, I thought, and how many lawyers named Kennedy were there in New England?

"Thank you, Nora, for telling me about Rosie. It helps."

"Are you sure I can't interest you in a night cream for those dark circles under your eyes? I've got one that clears them up in three weeks...tops."

Didn't I wish.

"Maybe another time," I told her and hurried back the way I had come, through the maze of fluorescent lights and obnoxious smells until I was out the door and mercifully in the realm of fresh air and natural sunlight again.

Now I'd have to find a lawyer named Kennedy who once had longish brown hair and wore cheap suits. Talk about the proverbial needle in a haystack. Why had Rosie never mentioned him to me?

Chapter Fourteen

While I'd been gone, Bud had packed the car for our Memorial Day weekend trip to his small cottage in Portsmouth. As I threw a few personal items into a bag, he got Casey into the car and double-checked that all the lights were off, the coffee pot was unplugged, and the garbage had been taken out.

It was maybe an hour's ride to Bud's two-bedroom, white clapboard bungalow that sat on the water. The area was quiet, with similar homes built only yards from each other and crowded onto a narrow beach. Trees, scattered along the single-lane blacktop road, wound in between the homes. Small green lawns in front of each structure sloped down to a band of stones, then mud, then sand, and finally the cold, gray Atlantic itself.

White Adirondack chairs dotted the lawns, a safer location than the sand as the New England tides are fierce and long — exposing maybe 150 yards of beach at low tide and lapping the stone-edged lawns at high. The small community, located where the Piscataqua River joins the Atlantic Ocean, felt like a step back into the 1950s, with Toyota Camrys seeming out of place with the architecture and, unfortunately, some of the attitudes.

It was cozy in that small-town way that disliked strangers and used gossip as entertainment. The men wore, what my friends laughingly called, "wife beater" underwear shirts, and the women still did housework in curlers during the day. Bud was the exception to the stranger rule; law enforcement personnel were always welcome.

While not the cedar-shingled retreat of the rich one imagines on Martha's Vineyard, it was quiet, it was on the water, and it was all Bud could afford on his small-town cop's retirement pay.

The living room of Bud's cottage featured a mural on one wall of a sandy beach with palm trees and lush tropical flowers. His friends and family had bought him every possible "life is a beach" accessory from wall plaques to dish towels to martini glasses shaped like palm trees.

He kept a skiff on the front lawn and liked to spend hours moored just outside the breakers with his fishing pole in the water and his eyes closed in contentment. I sat on the lawn and read and refilled his vodka and tonic as needed.

If the weather was cool in the afternoon, we'd sit on green overstuffed chairs and play video games as the sun reflected off the water and the cares of the week melted away. At four, we would retire to the Florida room with its view of the cold Atlantic and drink cocktails until dinnertime.

For dinner, we'd drive into Portsmouth to eat at one of the many taverns lining the harbor. The seafood was always scrumptious, the beer cold, and the music old-time rock 'n roll. Bud didn't dance, but once in a while, I'd have a little too much to drink and stand up in between the tables and do a little pony or cha-cha just for fun.

If we both had too much to drink, we'd stand up and do our version of a slow dance, clinging to each other and shuffling our feet, enjoying the honky-tonk romance of the night.

Some weekends, this weekend being one of them, Bud would wake up on a Sunday morning with back pain from an old injury he received in the Vietnam War. When that happened, he'd take a strong painkiller, and we'd plan to spend the day in bed. His bed was a king-sized island with a battered old mattress and padded headboard. With just a few extra pillows we could comfortably camp out there for the whole day — eating, reading, and watching TV.

On these mornings, I'd run out to the corner store for the Sunday papers and come back to find Bud fixing pancakes, bacon, and sausage, which we'd take into the bedroom and eat while watching the Sunday morning talking heads.

Bud would be on my right all tangled up in the jungle-print sheets, Casey would be on my left begging for another piece of bacon, and I would sit in the middle of them stuffing my face with pancakes and thinking that I hadn't been this happy in a long, long time.

I usually said a little prayer of gratitude at this point, not wanting the powers-that-be to think I took all this for granted, for which sin I might need to be punished by taking it all away.

It wasn't until our drive back to Swansea on Monday evening that I brought up the topic of the mysterious lawyer Rosie had been meeting on the night before she died.

"Do you know if there are a lot of personal injury lawyers in Swansea?" I asked after telling him about my trip to Lacy's and conversation with Nora. "The last name might be Kennedy."

"There're not a lot, actually," he said. "The most likely candidate would be Orvus Kennedy. He handles a lot of auto accidents. He does rather well. He's also got the reputation of being quite the womanizer. The cops hate him."

"Why?"

"Because he's so good at twisting your words. I testified in court once for the prosecution. The woman who caused the accident was clearly in the wrong, but by the time Orvus was done with me, I couldn't be sure of my own name."

"So I guess his client won."

"Yes and no. She won that day, but she just went on to cause another accident a few years later and lost her life. Luckily, she didn't take anybody with her."

"He's still in town?"

"Oh, yeah. Has an office on High Street. Tell him Bud says 'Hi.'"

Chapter Fifteen: Tuesday

When I went to work Tuesday morning, I had a meeting with Joan D'Angelo, my immediate boss and supervisor for the new customer service reps. She and I had a superficially friendly relationship, but underneath there were unhappy feelings left over from a training trip we'd taken together earlier in the year and a subsequent issue of my refusing to train a night class.

Joan was a largish woman with shoulder-length blonde hair that hung in a soft frame around her pale face. I'd say she was five feet ten, 180 pounds, with most of that weight stored in her upper arms and chest. Her wide shoulders and protruding bosom gave off the vibe of a bully. She wore conservative skirts and suit jackets, no makeup, and no jewelry.

Her office was also plain: two movable, gray walls placed perpendicular to an outside wall, creating a three-sided room with a large wood desk that faced away from a small window. A couple of padded wood chairs faced the desk, and the wall to the right held a low, gray metal filing cabinet.

The only decorations were plaques on a wall chronicling Joan's career: three for Employee of the Month, two for Supervisor of the Month, and one white document emblazoned with gold ink saying Quality Customer Service.

I saw no framed photos of husband or child, though I knew she had both, and no prints or paintings on the walls. Her office was all very cold and impersonal, much like the persona Joan herself strove to present. She could have been the spokesperson for the modern business woman.

"How are the new recruits?" she asked.

"Most are doing well. We have a few with prior experience who are setting a wonderful example for the newbies."

"I'd like them to start sitting with people on the floor this week. Do you think they're ready?"

"Oh yes, I think they need that."

"I've been hearing stories from some of your trainees about one person who's struggling...Grace."

"Well, yes, she has a little longer learning curve than some of the others, but she's really trying hard. I'm sure with practice she'll be fine."

"Don't hesitate to let me know," she said. "We can always replace her."

I had no doubt.

"Here's a list," she continued, "of the reps you can use to partner with the trainees. I'll check in on you midweek."

"Okay, thanks," I said and left. Would Grace pass muster? I had my doubts.

I walked out to the floor where the customer service reps were arranged in circular pods, six reps to a pod, with about four feet of desktop between each computer. The walls of the pods were gray padded sheets of metal that hooked together with u-shaped metal clasps. It was all very industrial looking.

Six was a pretty close fit, and each rep could overhear the surrounding conversations. Most of the reps wore headphones with a microphone that arced out from the headset to float just inches from their mouth, thus the customer couldn't hear the noise in the pod.

The headphones also automatically forwarded each caller to a rep, alerting the rep with a loud beep to stop talking to a neighbor and greet the customer. A few reps, like Claire, still used the old fashioned setup of a phone that rang and had to be answered, but most found that arrangement too cumbersome. It was much easier to use the keyboard with hands free.

I spoke to each of the reps on the list and explained that I'd be bringing out a trainee to sit with them. I assigned the kindest and most patient rep to Grace.

"Pat," I told her, "I'm going to have Grace sit with you. She's having some difficulty in class, but I know you're very organized, and maybe you can share some of your best practices to help her succeed."

Pat was older and had three or four grown children, so I hoped she'd take Grace under her wing and teach her tricks to survive not only the demanding customers but also the demanding managers who basically wanted callers made happy and off the line as fast as possible.

It was all about the numbers, how many calls a rep took per day and tracking how many calls were transferred up the line to supervisors. Pleasing a customer is pretty hard with management breathing down your neck, and pleasing management when customers need soothing and cajoling to keep them from canceling their card is even harder. It's a very hard job to do well.

When placing Martha, I chose a young man with an Australian accent who was one of our star performers. Brian called all the customers "mate" and never failed to inquire about how they were feeling or what the weather was like where they lived. By the time the customers got around to their reason for calling, half would decide not to bother the nice gentleman with their minor problem, which they were sure would clear itself up by the next statement. Since Martha had already mastered all the systems and procedures, I thought she was ready to hone her verbal skills by observing Brian. She seemed to know who he was already and gave me a wink as I left. It was such a pleasure to have a trainee who was already on top of the game.

On my lunch break, I called the office of Orvus Kennedy. Surprisingly, he answered the phone himself.

"Orvus Kennedy, attorney," he announced after only one ring.

"Hi, I'm Emily Menotti. I'm calling to ask you about a friend of mine that you were working with a few years ago. Her name was Rose Hamlin. She died suddenly of a heart attack. Do you remember her?"

"Most assuredly," he said. "What's the nature of your concern?"

"I'd actually like to make an appointment to talk to you about her. I'm not thinking of taking any legal action, but I'll be glad to pay your fee for a consultation."

"We'll talk about that when I see you. What's a good time?"

"Well, I'm a trainer and I can't really take time off during the day. Do you have evening office hours?"

"Usually, but they get booked pretty fast. How about a week from this Tuesday, June 8th, at 7 p.m.?"

"Wonderful. Can I have your address?"

"Twenty-eight B High Street, up a few stairs from the street. You'll see my name on the door."

"Thank you so much!"
"Looking forward to it," he said and hung up. I could hardly wait.

Chapter Sixteen

When I finally dragged myself home at the end of the day, I found Bud's car missing. As I let myself in the door, Casey was there to greet me. I sat down on the floor and hugged him, loving the feel of his nose on my face and his big warm body slumped down in my lap. If it wasn't good for my allergies, it was certainly good for my soul.

On the kitchen table, I found a note. "Visiting Tanya," it read. "Home for dinner. Kisses."

I made my way upstairs and changed into jeans and a sweatshirt. This was a custom-made sweatshirt Bud had ordered especially for me. It had a screen print on the front from a photo he'd taken of me, sitting on the floor as I'd just done, with my arms around Casey. Underneath the picture, words said "True Love."

I was just coming back down the stairs when Bud's car pulled into the driveway. I went to the door to greet him.

"How's Tanya?" I asked after a quick kiss.

"Not good. She stayed home from work today. Says she's too depressed to get out of bed. She says if she doesn't get out of bed, then she can't lose anything. So she just sits there with the TV on all day. She says the TV drowns out the voices."

He took off his coat, and I hung it in the closet for him.

"Hearing voices is serious stuff. She really needs professional help."

He went to the fridge and pulled out vodka and olives to make himself a martini.

"She can't go. She says the department will force her to take a desk job if they find out she's seeing a shrink. She seems to think she just needs rest. I don't know what to tell her, except that I'm here for her to talk to anytime she needs me."

As he talked, I took two glasses out of the cabinet, a martini glass with painted palm trees for him and a flower-painted wine glass for me.

"Poor thing. What do you think she needs?"

He mixed the vodka, a quick splash of vermouth, and a teaspoon of the olive juice in the shaker. Then he added ice.

"I'm stumped," he said, as he began shaking the mixture. "And her house is a mess. She claims something is moving her things. Something paranormal."

I got a bottle of wine from the fridge. Items moving reminded me of Derek's complaint, but I didn't see how the two could be connected.

"Maybe she should call in a psychic investigator."

"No." He slammed the shaker on the countertop so hard its vibration nearly knocked over our glasses.

I continued pouring my wine while he poured out his cocktail.

"That's all nonsense and you know it. I don't care that you waste your own time with it, but you won't waste Tanya's."

"Understood," I said, and walked out of the kitchen.

It took him a few minutes to join me in the living room. I didn't want to continue the disagreement. I hoped he felt the same.

He sat down next to me on the sofa where I was watching the six o'clock news. "Sorry," he said. "I'm just upset about my daughter."

"I understand. Let's hope that rest is what she needs."

"Chicken and rice for dinner?"

"Wonderful."

Chapter Seventeen: Friday

Melinda and I went back to the old mill that Friday. She picked me up at nine thirty, just as Bud was going upstairs for the night. He kissed me good-bye and warned me to be careful.

I told him not to worry, but to be honest, I wasn't sure if maybe he should worry a little. I had a bad feeling about the evening, a little unhappiness in the pit of my stomach that I often get when my gut is trying to warn me that I might be making a mistake. I remembered the time I'd had that feeling just before I put a letter in the mailbox that I later regretted sending, and the time I accepted a second date with someone about whose character I had doubts. That little warning was rarely wrong.

Rain was falling, so the residents had gone to a local hotel for the evening. There was something especially depressing about approaching the dark structure amid heavy drops of cold rain and the occasional gust of icy wind. The calendar might have read early June, but that night, it felt like December.

As before, the SRBPS was already there; the time was about ten o'clock. Melinda and I jumped from her SUV and ran to the large black van where the technicians and investigators were planning their forays into the building.

The crew consisted of six men and one woman—and Melinda and me. What's always surprising to me about ghost investigators is how normal they look. Ghost hunting seems like such an out-of-the-ordinary job, that you'd expect some equally out-of-the-ordinary participants, but that wasn't true for this group. The men had mostly short haircuts and wore conservative jeans and dark tee shirts, along with dark-colored windbreakers.

The one girl was of medium build and sturdy looking, with short, spiky, dyed black hair and small, wire rim glasses. She was dressed exactly like the guys in jeans and dark jacket. They all blended in so completely with the night that they appeared to be a natural part of it, one and the same with the shadowy figures they were seeking.

"We've got two cameras set up in the first floor entrance hall to ensure no one enters without our knowledge."

James was speaking and explaining what was planned for the night.

"There's another focused on the stairway and a fourth in unit number seven, Derek Smith's bedroom, where he claims to have seen a mist appear at the foot of his bed. The last one is in the attic, again to make sure no one is lurking around and to check for stray birds and animals that might have made their home there."

Lots of supposedly paranormal activity often turned out to be squirrels and raccoons trapped in the attic. Likewise, critters in the cellar could screech and growl to the alarm of the naïve. Luckily, this structure had no basement.

"What are people reporting?" a tech named Bill asked.

"All the usual things...like footsteps, loud noises, and low whispers. Derek is the only one who says he saw a mist. He also claims that items move around on their own. Some of the other residents claim to be brushed on the stairway by someone they can't see. But there've been no reports of physical attacks or injuries."

I knew from speaking to Melinda that, in the past, ghost investigators have had their hair pulled, arms scratched, and some even pushed down the stairs.

"Ed and Alison will go in first with the handheld cameras and the EMF detector..." James looked at me, "that's, electromagnetic field detector," then resumed, "I think they should cover the first floor and the attic. When they return, Robert and I will go in and explore the second floor. Steve and Bill will stay in the van and monitor the computers. We'll decide what to do next after everyone's reported back about their experiences. Scott, of course, will join both groups as the videographer."

"Melinda, if you don't mind, I'll have you accompany both teams and let me know what you experience."

"Can Emily come too?" asked Melinda.

"Maybe on the second floor walk-through," James said. "Now, first, everyone check to make sure their equipment has fresh batteries."

There was silence as the crew examined their flashlights, cameras, and other devices to make sure they were operating properly and had plenty of power.

I found myself a seat on a camp stool in the largest van and watched with the others as Ed, Allison, Melinda, and the videographer, laden with backpacks stuffed with cameras and other recording devices, moved en masse beneath huge black umbrellas to trudge through the downpour. When they reached the small overhang that sheltered the front door, they huddled there while they closed their umbrellas and unpacked and shouldered their equipment. They slowly pushed the door open and focused their cameras into the gloom.

I turned from watching them in person to watching them on the computer, which had a thirty-two-inch screen divided into six squares to take feeds from six different cameras. Five were assigned to the mounted cameras, and the sixth could be switched to the feeds from the different handheld cameras.

Having seen this part of an investigation countless times on TV, I found watching it on the monitors a little bit difficult and even boring. There's only so many times you can hear an investigator say "Is anyone there?" or "Is there anyone who wants to speak to us?" At some point, you mentally check out from the one-sided conversation and start focusing your attention on the dark corners of the camera images, where you hope to catch a door opening on its own or a shadowy figure moving from one doorway to another.

After sixty minutes of slowly entering each room of the six first-floor condos and then the attic, and after taking multiple EVP readings that were always at zero, James called the van on his communicator to see if they had picked up anything on the cameras and audio equipment.

"Nothing," Steve said. "Not even footsteps."

The group took a break at this point. Back in the van, they unpacked sandwiches and sodas from coolers. The breather was low-key, with whispered conversations and muffled laughs. Steve and Bill kept an eye on the computer monitors as we ate ham and cheese sandwiches and potato chips. We drank Coca Colas because no alcohol was allowed.

"What do you think, Mel?" I asked.

"I don't know. I haven't really picked up on any individual spirit trying to make contact. Maybe we'll be luckier on the second floor."

After the half-hour break, James said, "Next team," and he motioned to Robert, a small man with a neatly trimmed brown goatee. Melinda and I joined them, along with Scott. Melinda and I shared one of the huge umbrellas and the guys another. I shivered a bit as we marched together across the lawn. It was still raining pretty hard, but luckily, there was no lightning. This wasn't an early summer thunderstorm; it was a cold, steady downpour.

James carried an infrared camera, and Robert the EMF detector. Both carried walkie-talkies that connected them to Steve and Bill in the van.

As we entered, you could immediately feel the air change. Though damp and heavy outside, inside the atmosphere was dry but somehow thicker, like we were pushing through dense, other-worldly vegetation.

Melinda immediately commented, "Do you feel it? There's something that's disturbed by our being here. I didn't notice it on the first trip in."

We walked slowly toward the steps to the second floor, James discovering the way through his camera's viewfinder. No flashlights were permitted unless absolutely necessary. I tried to stay as close to Melinda as I could, following the dim light of the camera. We made an awkward quintet, trying not to bump into each other as we clumsily climbed the wooden steps.

We started on the right at condo number twelve. The residents had left all their doors unlocked, and I imagine had taken any money and other moveable valuables with them. Derek's unit was number seven and we were leaving it for last.

We slowly opened the door, and as our eyes adjusted to the darkness, I noticed that, with the little bit of diffused light that came from the parking lot outside and the glow from James's camera, we could just make out the shapes of the living room furniture. The air was a little lighter in here, and as we moved from dining room to kitchen to bedrooms to baths, we noted no unusual sights or sounds.

"Feels okay to me," Melinda said. "I don't detect any threats or presences trying to make themselves known."

We sat on the sofa in the living room and on the beds in the bedrooms, again with James or Robert repeating, "Is there anyone here? Is there anyone who wants to speak to us?" Occasionally they would change it to "Did you used to work here when it was a mill?

Did you die here?" Like any manual labor force in the early days of the industrial revolution, many who were sick, weak, or careless died. Perhaps their spirits were trying to communicate.

This process repeated itself with the next four units, and I was beginning to get just a little tired and cranky with our lack of success. How did these guys do this for hours and hours at house after house without totally giving up? I really had to admire their perseverance.

After closing the door on unit number eight, I glanced at the lighted dial of my watch and saw that it was now 3 a.m.

James said, "Derek's condo is next. Melinda, let me know what you feel."

We were back to the top of the steps and door number seven. Melinda turned the knob and we slowly entered.

As James pointed his camera to various spots in Derek's living room, you could see the usual leather furniture and stacked TV and stereo devices that males so love.

Robert said, "EMFs are up. I've got a reading of 2.5...no 7.5... Wow, we're up to 20!"

I was excited. Escalating numbers are usually an indication of paranormal activity.

Melinda spoke up. "Someone's here. Someone female. She's crying."

"Rosie," I whispered. Out of the corner of my eye I thought I saw movement in the dining area.

"Whoa!" cried James softly, who turned and pointed his camera in that direction. Everyone halted.

"EMFs are spiking. We're up to forty." said Robert.

"Who's got the digital recorder?" James asked.

"I do," Melinda whispered. "It's on."

Scott swung his video camera around the room.

"The crying is coming from the bedroom," Melinda said. Without asking each other, we all started walking in that direction.

"I hear it," I said, as a soft sobbing filled the room. I also noticed that the air temperature had dropped hugely—maybe twenty or thirty degrees. We were all shivering, and not just from fear.

"We hear it too," James and Robert whispered in unison.

"Rosie, is that you?" I asked.

There was a crash, and James yelled, "There!" I saw him point to a table by the bed. A heavy, cut-glass lamp with a flowered shade lay on its side.

"Why are you here?" I asked, and suddenly a book flew from a shelf on the far wall and landed on the floor. Then another, and another, until all the books on the shelf were on the floor. I was terrified, but aware that none of the books had been aimed at any of us. Still, I stepped back a bit into the doorway, worried that we were in danger.

"Are you getting this?" James asked Scott.

"Damned straight I am."

"Is this Rosie?" Melinda asked. I didn't answer, but I could have told her it was. It felt just like her, like when she was angry, when she would accuse me of not understanding her. Her tension and frustration were palpable.

Then we heard noises in the kitchen, and we all hurried there. We stopped in the doorway as cabinet door after cabinet door was opened, and the cabinets' contents were sent flying through the air. Dumbstruck, we watched as glasses, cups, plates levitated and shot forward to the middle of the room, only to suddenly lose momentum and fall to the floor where they shattered into a hundred tiny pieces. Derek would not be happy. Again, none of the objects came close enough to hurt us.

Melinda spoke up, "It's okay, Rosie, we're here. We're listening. We want to understand. Let us tell your story."

Then we heard noises from the living room. We hurried to reach the entryway and watched in the dim glow of the outdoor lighting as record albums, eight tracks, cassette tapes, and videos were hurtled through the air, almost as if someone were looking for something and tossing these out of the way. Once again, none of the objects seemed to be aimed at us.

When that activity ended, we heard a cabinet across the room rattling. James took out a small flashlight and shined it in that direction. The cabinet had glass doors that were shaking as if someone were trying to open them. The cabinet housed a display of Star Trek: The Next Generation figurines and memorabilia. After a few seconds, the doors burst open and the miniature figures of Captain Picard, Commanders Troi, Data, and all the Enterprise crew began to get the same treatment as the books, the kitchenware, and the audiotapes. We were almost nonchalant watching it now, having seen this activity three times before. If we weren't so dumbstruck, we might have laughed.

James spoke softly to us that he'd never seen such deliberate and continuous paranormal activity as he was seeing tonight. He was thrilled to be a witness to it.

All of a sudden something dropped at my feet. I jumped, frightened out of my wits that an object had been hurled so close to me. James picked it up and turned it over in his free hand. It looked like a small TV remote control, but it had too few buttons. All activity suddenly ceased.

Melinda, excited, said, "For some reason, this is important. The spirit wants us to notice it."

James, examining the object closely, said, "It's a phaser from the Star Trek stuff. See, there are the two settings...stun and kill. It's set to kill."

After a pause, he continued, "What could the spirit possibly mean by a phaser? Did it want us to notice the settings, stun and kill, and more especially 'kill'? If it had wanted to kill Derek, presumably it would have tried to by now, but all Derek has reported was seeing a mist and objects moving."

"Is she trying to tell us that Derek killed her?" I asked.

"Could be," Melinda offered.

The unit was quiet now and the atmosphere had changed. The air was lighter.

Melinda said, "She's gone."

Robert said, "So are the EMF readings."

"We can go now," James said and led the team to the door and down the steps. "We'll see what the guys in the van got and then we'll listen to the audiotape. But even if we don't get anything else, tonight was wicked good. This is one of most successful investigations I've ever led. Good work, guys."

As we exited the building, we noticed that the rain had stopped, and we could see the first rosy shades of dawn edging up on the eastern horizon. I was exhausted, but anxious to see what other evidence the tech team had picked up.

As we found seats in the van, Melinda rewound the tape and then pushed Play. At first there was silence except for the team whispering to each other and commenting on the lack of activity. Melinda fast-forwarded the tape up to where we were about to enter Derek's unit. Then we heard the crying. It was sad and eerie together. One or two places, though, the crying stopped, and an unintelligible whisper could be heard. Melinda rewound the tape and amplified it. It was still scratchy, but it sounded like a female voice pleading, "Not that, please, not that."

"Do you think Derek hurt Rosie?" I asked. "Are we hearing her begging him not to hit her?"

"We can't say anything for sure," James cautioned. "We can't verify that it's Rosie speaking. This may be just a residual haunting that began any time in the past 200, or so, years. The spirit could be someone who died in the old mill, and whose voice just replays itself over and over for anyone to hear. An EVP isn't really proof of anything without hard evidence."

"And the mist Derek saw?" I asked.

"Could be the same person who died in the mill. But the activity we saw, the objects flying out of cabinets and across the room, that's evidence of an active haunting. Someone is sending us a message seeming to say he or she was killed."

"What do we do next?"

"We let our technical team examine all the evidence we caught tonight, from all the cameras and all the recorders, and put it together for us to review. It'll be ready in three or four days...we all have day jobs. But I'll be in touch when I have something to show you."

Melinda found her purse and took out her car keys, indicating that she was ready to leave. I was grateful we had done this on a Friday night so I could catch up on a little sleep in the morning before Bud and I got started on our Saturday chores.

As I climbed into the SUV, I said, "Thank you so much for letting me be a part of this tonight. What an experience! I was scared and excited all at the same time."

I said to Melinda, "I don't know how much Bud will believe it, but I feel like I'm justified in suspecting that Rosie's death was not just a random heart attack."

"I agree," Melinda replied. "That was some pissed-off spirit, and she wants vindication. Do you think Derek is in some way responsible?"

"Well, why else would she be so active in Derek's home and not mine?"

"I didn't tell you before because I didn't want to scare you, but I've see an apparition in your home."

"What? You have? When? Why haven't I seen her?"

"It was that night I came by and then Tanya came. I saw something on your front porch, a mist that couldn't be explained by the weather. It was hovering around the front window like it was watching you. Maybe it was afraid to come in."

"Afraid? A ghost afraid of me?"

"Or Bud. He has a powerful animus. His spirit might be warding off others in an effort to protect you. He wouldn't know about it consciously. It would be happening without his awareness."

"Well, now that I think about it, maybe that's okay. Even though I wanted to go on the SRBPS investigation, I'm not too confident about dealing with the paranormal in my own home. I told you about what I saw at the Laundromat and the phone message at work. So I guess Rosie is trying to get in touch with me. But I still think Derek had something to do with her death. I do have another lead, though."

I told Melinda about my appointment with Orvus Kennedy.

"Maybe he'll have some answers for me."

We drove the rest of the way home in silence, for which I was glad. I reviewed the night's activity over and over in my mind. Rosie's death was a homicide, I had no doubt of it, and Derek was my first suspect. Why else would he have seen the mist at the foot of his bed? He was involved, and I was hoping to find out how.

Chapter Eighteen: Saturday

On Saturday, Bud and I slept in until eight o'clock. Then we had a quick breakfast of cereal, coffee, and juice, followed by our regular chores and shopping. I still hadn't talked to him about the investigation at the Old Mill. I knew he wasn't sympathetic, but then few would be.

As we were walking in the door with our bags of groceries, the phone in the living room was ringing. Bud picked it up and said hello and, after a pause said, "She's right here. I'll let you talk to her."

I gave him a questioning look, wondering who it was, but he just handed me the phone and said, "For you." There was an edge to his voice that let me know he wasn't happy about who it was on the other end of the line.

"Hello?"

"Hi, Em, it's Derek. Got a sec?"

"Sure. What's happening?"

"One of the investigators told me what went on in my condo last night. I guess he thought I'd be sore when I saw the mess. I'm not angry, but I'd like to talk to you about it."

"No problem. I have some time. Come on over."

"Well, if you don't mind, I'd like to talk to you in private. Can you meet me in that bar down by the waterfront, the Crucifixion whatever? I don't think anybody I know will be there on a Saturday afternoon."

I hesitated. This would be a tough one to explain to Bud, but I really wanted to ask Derek some questions.

"Okay, how about I meet you in fifteen minutes?"

"See you then," he said and disconnected.

I went out to the car and grabbed the last bag of groceries and a box of wine. Bud closed the trunk and asked, "What was that about?" Again, he sounded a little pissed off.

"That was Derek. We had some problems in his condo last night. Books and dishes and knickknacks came flying off his shelves by themselves and broke on the floor. He's not too happy about it."

"You're kidding me, right? You don't think those weird ghosty guys rigged the whole thing to suck you into their spirit-hunting scam?"

"No, I don't. And I'm hurt that you think I'm so stupid that I'd allow myself to get pulled into something like that. These are sincere guys, trying to help people make sense of things outside of their normal experience."

"Well, I don't believe any of it. Are you running over there now to do some more investigating?" I knew what he was implying and, now, I was angry.

"I'm meeting him downtown, at the same bar where I first met you. Do you want to come along?"

"So he wants to enlist your help with his paranormal experiences and maybe get your assistance with some of his other loser-guy problems?"

That was it. I picked up my purse and headed for the door.

"See you later," was all I said and left.

The Crucifixion Bar and Grill was a dive on Third Street, just half a block up from the waterfront. The wind that forever blew off the water created a bone-numbing chill in the winter, but a refreshingly cool breeze in the summer.

I easily found a parking spot on the cobblestoned street and enjoyed the scent of the cool air as I made my way to the tavern. I was still fuming inside at Bud, but that was soon overridden by my interest in what Derek had to say. Had he done something to Rosie to cause her death? I had to ask questions.

When I entered the dimly lit room, I immediately saw Derek sitting at the bar hunched over a mug of beer. I went over and sat on the stool beside him, and he gave me a half-grin that seemed to spring from embarrassment.

"Let's get a table," he said, picking up his beer and getting up from his seat. We weaved around empty tables and chairs to a spot in the corner. I wasn't quite sure what he was aiming at—not to be seen himself or not to be seen with me.

I had barely settled myself down when he blurted out, "What the hell happened last night, Em? I never had spirits throwing dishes and things all over the place. What did you guys do?

Provoke a firefight in my dining room?"

"I thought you'd reported objects moving and a mist appearing in your home?"

"Well, yeah. I found some pictures turned around to face the wall...pictures of me and Martha...and I did see a white thing at the foot of my bed, but nothing ever went flying through the air. Nothing was ever broken."

"I can't explain what happened. All I can tell you is that I witnessed what was caught on the videotape. The books in your bedroom, the dishes in the kitchen, and your Star Trek stuff were all thrown about by someone or something that I don't understand either. Melinda and I speculated that it was Rosie's spirit trying to communicate with the investigators, but James and his crew said it could just as well have been the spirits of dead mill workers. Of course, they didn't know Rosie. Is there anything about what you saw that makes you think Rosie would be involved?"

"She's dead, Em. How could she be involved? I thought it might be something like tremors, or electromagnetic fields, or gases coming up from the ground. I'm not so sure I buy into the paranormal explanation."

The waitress came by at this point and asked me what I wanted to drink. As I recalled from my previous visit, their selection of wine ran to two choices: red or white.

"A glass of white wine, please," I told her, and she quickly vanished. "Can I ask you exactly what happened when you and Rosie broke up?"

"Well, we had one hell of a fight. And I still don't understand why she got so upset." This sounded familiar.

"I surprised her with reservations to one of those fantasy hotels...you know, the kind where you can rent a suite of rooms to resemble a Gothic castle, or a southern plantation, or even a jungle. I suggested the Hugh Hefner Mansion with a hot tub and a round bed, complete with a silk smoking jacket for me and a Playboy Bunny costume for her." He paused, remembering the conversation.

Then he continued, "Rosie absolutely exploded, called me a scumbag and a fascist pig, and said she'd have me and the hotel management arrested for distributing pornography...I mean, what was that about? We're all adults. The hotel wasn't providing nude videos, although now that I think about it, maybe I could have asked..."

"Derek, back on track here. Then what happened?"

He didn't say anything as the waitress deposited a brandy snifter of dusky yellow liquid in front of me. She lingered for a moment to see if it was okay. To be polite, I faked a sip and told her it was fine.

When she was out of earshot, Derek went on, "Rosie went to the bedroom where she kept clothes for when she spent the night and started throwing lingerie and nighties at me and screaming, 'Is that all you men ever think about? Sex, sex, and more sex?' So I said, 'Well, yes, to be truthful, that is all we think about.'"

"Wrong answer," I said.

"I knew that, but she was being unreasonable and I wanted to show her two could play that game. Then she went into a rant about all the men she'd ever dated and what dirtballs we all were and she was done with it. She was done with me, she was done with dating, and she was packing her things and leaving."

"Did you try to stop her?"

"I tried to kiss her. I tried to tell her how sexy she looked when she was angry. It had worked before. This time it didn't."

"Did you hit her?"

"No, of course not. I'm not into hitting women. She shoved me to get me out of her way, but I didn't respond physically."

"Did she fall down or hurt herself in the process of getting her things together and leaving?"

"No. She just threw the lingerie into that oversized purse of hers, grabbed a few items out of the bathroom, and slammed out the door."

"Did you or she say anything else before she left?"

"Yeah, she shouted, 'You'll be sorry,' and I shouted back, 'I doubt it.' Then she slammed the door and I never saw her again."

"Did you ever notice any odd marks on her abdomen? Little black marks right about here?" I pointed to the right middle of my stomach.

"No, why?"

"She had those when she died...I don't know how she got them. Did you know the coroner said she died of a heart attack?"

"No, I didn't know that. That's too bad. We'd been split up a while when she died. I never really gave it much thought."

"Did she ever complain of heart trouble or pains in her chest?"

"Not that I recall. I don't remember Rosie ever being sick to tell you the truth."

I sipped the wine, buying time while I thought. I didn't remember

Rosie ever being sick either. The wine wasn't half bad, probably a chardonnay, but not something I'd choose if I had more options.

"She didn't ever talk about her family, like how her parents died or anything like that?"

"No, not at all. We didn't talk about our families. I was an only child of parents who were only children, so I didn't have a family to talk about."

Derek seemed to be telling the truth as far as I could tell. He wasn't exhibiting any of those telltale signs they say liars have like fidgeting or looking away. I wished I'd thought to bring Melinda. She was good at sussing out an aura of deceit.

"Back to our original topic, Em. You really think it was Rosie's ghost throwing all the objects around in my condo?"

"I can't say for sure, but when I was in there, it just felt like Rosie. I don't know what her problem was, but she sometimes overreacted to things in a paranoid kind of way and was totally selfish about her own feelings while sometimes running roughshod over others. I felt that same frightful, almost spinning-out-of-control anger that I'd seen in her before. But I've no proof, so I don't know what to tell you."

"So I guess I just wait and see what happens next?"

"If what happened last night happens again, I'm sure the investigators can put you in touch with someone that can help. The woman with me, Melinda, might have some suggestions. Do you want her phone number?"

"No, I'll tough it out a bit longer. I'll see if anything goes on tonight. It just all seems a bit unreal."

Derek appeared genuinely honest and befuddled. Considering this, I put a big question mark next to his name in my mind. He hadn't left town since Rosie had died or done anything suspicious. And if he had harmed her, I didn't think he would have been open to having the SRBPS investigate his home.

"I should be going, Derek. My boyfriend is probably imagining the worst. The SRBPS will be back in touch with the results of their investigation."

"Thanks for seeing me, Em. I've got your wine on my tab. Take care of yourself."

"You too, Derek," and I got up and left.

As I walked to my car I was thinking that, although he now seemed an unlikely suspect, I had discovered Derek could be a decent guy on occasion.

CHAPTER NINETEEN

When I got home, Bud was in a surprisingly good mood. I found him sitting on the deck, sipping a vodka and tonic, throwing a ball out into the yard for Casey, and waiting patiently while he found it and brought it back. Casey gave his usual bark of happiness when he saw me.

"How'd it go?"

"Well, Derek's not so much angry at what happened as wanting to know why. I really couldn't help him too much with that. I don't understand why either. We talked about Rosie and why they broke up and if he knew anything about health problems that might have led to her having a heart attack. He couldn't tell me anything. I'm very discouraged."

"Maybe you should just let it go. Your friend is dead of natural causes. There's nothing else to be done."

I decided not to argue with him, but that didn't mean I was giving up my investigation.

"Did you get any lunch?" he asked.

"No, I never got around to it. How about you?"

"I didn't either. It's three o'clock. How about we go out for an early dinner and then go to the movies. Maybe that will help you feel better."

I hadn't been to the movies since Bud and I had started dating. He wasn't a big fan of what he called the "walk-ins," so I was surprised and touched that he was offering to go.

"Great," I said. "I need to freshen up a bit. I'll be ready in ten minutes."

We went to Applebee's where I ordered my current fave, Pecan Crusted Chicken Salad. Bud had his usual, Jack Daniels Barbecued Steak. I enjoyed my Pinot Grigio; Bud, his vodka tonic.

We lingered over dinner and even shared a piece of carrot cake, waiting for the movie theater to open at five.

Our little cinema was often a year behind the first run movies, but since it was the only theater in town, there was always an audience. Tonight's flick, *Fight Club*, starred Brad Pitt, Edward Norton, Helena Bonham Carter, and Meatloaf. I'd heard it was a great film and was intrigued by the title.

About one-third of the way through the movie, when it seemed that the action was going to be just one brutal fight after another, Bud said he didn't like it and wanted to leave. I wanted to stay. Even though I'm not a fan of big screen violence, I wondered how it would end.

And the action supposedly took place in Wilmington, Delaware, my hometown and the center of most bank credit card operations in the 1980s and '90s. Part of the movie plot was a plan to blow up the bank buildings. The bad guys erroneously thought that this would make everyone's credit card debt disappear. As I knew from having worked at Chase Manhattan in the eighties, every key stroke on the computer is saved and backed up multiple times at various locations. You could blow up every building in Wilmington, and you'd still get your monthly credit card bill.

I asked Bud if he could give the movie a little more time. As he squirmed in his seat, I thought about all the episodes of *The Sopranos* and *WWF Smackdown* I had suffered through in an effort to be companionable. Couldn't he be as obliging?

The movie was intriguing for another reason too. Something about the tormented main character reminded me of Tanya. She, also, was one of those burdened with trying to live up to an unrealistic ideal and then finding herself lacking.

After fifteen minutes, Bud leaned over to me and said he was leaving but I could stay if I wanted. All I had to do was call when the movie was over and he'd come pick me up.

Darn. I really didn't want to fight with him over *Fight Club*, and he'd taken me out to dinner in an attempt to apologize for his behavior over my meeting Derek.

I got up to leave.

On Sunday, Bud got a disturbing call from Tanya. I heard him talking to her in a very concerned tone. It sounded as if her confusion and depression was getting worse.

"I'm sure it will straighten itself out, honey," I heard him say. "Don't jump to conclusions. Maybe you should take a short vacation with Rick for a week or two and see if the problem doesn't disappear. Maybe being out of the house and getting some extra sleep will help. A change of scene could be therapeutic."

He was silent for a few moments and then he said the strangest thing, "No, I don't think you're being haunted. But you could always try prayer or talking to a minister. That certainly couldn't hurt."

When he hung up the phone, I asked him, "What's wrong? That was Tanya, wasn't it? Does she think she's being haunted?"

"Not you too! What is it with women? Why do you believe in all this who-doo, voo-doo nonsense? Why can't you just accept the explanation that medical science has provided? Tanya is having a psychological problem. She's stressed out. She's still hearing voices, only she says now they've gotten angrier. Maybe she does need to see a shrink."

"Hearing voices is schizophrenia, hon. What are the voices saying?"

"Something about what a bad person she is and that she's going to learn her lesson...I don't know...I don't understand it. I think she's just let the job get to her."

"How stressful can being a small-town policewoman be?" I asked, picturing Andy Griffith strolling down the streets of Mayberry with Opie in tow on their way to visit Aunt Bea.

Bud shot me a how-stupid-can-you-be look. "I can tell you, but you probably won't believe me. Big *and* small towns have a never ending stream of drunks, drug addicts, wife abusers, and child neglecters. The police are always the first called in to help. It's hugely depressing to see only the bad side of human nature day in and day out...and then be expected to solve everyone's problems."

I nodded to show him that I understood and gave him a hug to try to assuage his anger and let him know I was on his side. He was right. I was so caught up in my own little privileged world of good friends and a loving partner that I often forgot how distressing life can be for those not as lucky as myself. I was fortunate enough to have been born into a kind and responsible family and to have graduated from college. I never struggled with poverty, or abusive parents, or the kind of pain that leads to poor decisions and life-altering mistakes.

"I'm sorry for being so thoughtless, hon. I think your daughter should see a counselor or a psychiatrist. Given her job, it's important she be as mentally healthy as possible. Will you suggest that to her?"

"You know I don't believe in all that spilling-your-guts-on-a-couch stuff, but if it might help her, I'll suggest it. I'll call her tomorrow to see how she's doing."

I gave him another hug and said a silent prayer that Tanya would find an answer to her problems.

When I arrived at work on Monday, I immediately went out on the floor to see how my trainees were doing. Most were doing well and had already started taking calls with their mentors at their side. But when I got to Grace, I could see she was unhappy and discouraged.

"Thank you for calling Metrobank NH Inc. How can I help you?" she said in her tiny voice. I couldn't hear the customer on the other end of the conversation, but I could sense that the customer was unhappy.

"Please hold while I access that information," Grace said and then put the caller on hold.

"Quick, Pat," she said. "Where do I find the interest rate? This man says we're charging him too much."

Oh my, I thought. Finding the current interest rate was a basic task. Grace shouldn't have had to put the caller on hold to find it. She should have been able to access it on the computer while they were speaking.

Pat said, "Just press F1, Grace. There it is...in the left hand column."

Grace took the caller off hold. "It's 18.5 percent, Mr. Smith."

"That's highway robbery!" came a voice so loud even I could hear it through the headphones. "You guys are crooks! How can a person ever pay down their bill if you're going to charge them that much interest?"

"I don't know, sir," said Grace, which was one of the worst things she could have told him. "Just keep making your monthly payments on time each month, and your balance will eventually be paid down."

We could all hear as the caller's receiver was slammed down with a loud curse.

"Grace," Pat said. "Why didn't you tell him that he might

qualify for a lower rate? Why didn't you offer to review his payment history to see if he's been on time for the past two years? Then he might have qualified for a reduction."

"I don't know," said Grace, almost in tears. "I get too flustered. The customers are all so angry. It's so upsetting I can't think."

Pat looked at me and rolled her eyes as if to say, "She's hopeless."

Grace caught the look and burst out, "But I need this job. How else am I going to support my children?"

"Just calm down," I told her. "You'll get used to it. Just keep practicing. Where's the cheat-sheet I gave you with all the screen names and corresponding keys on the keyboard?"

"I guess I lost it."

"Well, I'll bring you another one. Just keep trying."

Then I gave her my best encouraging smile and walked away, only to see Joan D'Angelo motioning me into her office.

"If Grace hasn't improved by tomorrow," Joan announced, "she's gone."

"Couldn't you at least give her until the end of the week?" I was trying not to beg but it probably sounded like it.

"She's had two or three second chances already. This is it. May I remind you that you're in no position to ask for favors?"

The bitch! Well, there was nothing more I could do. Grace would sink or swim on her own. Then I remembered Claire.

"What about Claire Hunter? How is it she doesn't get fired? At least Grace's not out-and-out rude to the callers. She's just new and overwhelmed. She'll improve in time."

"Claire is none of your business," Joan said.

I was dying to say, "You're afraid of her, aren't you?" but that might have gotten me fired.

"I have a conference call," Joan said, her way of telling me to leave. I was glad to, but I knew I'd never ever see a promotion at Metrobank, if I stayed here, until the day they rolled me out on a gurney. Joan would probably fire Grace now just to spite me. My aggrieved sense of justice had only made things worse for both Grace and me. Would I ever learn to keep my mouth shut?

I was so upset by my lack of professionalism that I went back to my desk and did a quick survey of any items I might want to grab quickly when the security officer showed up at my desk to escort me out the door. That was when you knew the shit had really hit the fan.

When I finally got home that night and had poured my heart out to Bud, he kissed me tenderly and mixed me a chocolate peppermint martini. Then, while I sat on a kitchen chair and sipped on that, he massaged my neck and upper shoulders. It was heavenly.

"It'll be alright, sweetheart," he assured me.

"Do you think I should quit and just find something else?"

"No, hon, because you know what happens when you quit? You find out two months later that the person you couldn't get along with has left the bank for a better job in a different city and all your worry was for naught. Just hang in there. I know it'll be alright."

I was only too glad to hope he was right.

Chapter Twenty: Tuesday

The next morning, as Bud showered and I was getting dressed for work, the phone rang. I answered it and recognized Tanya's voice right away. I also recognized the catch in her voice that told me she'd been crying.

"Hi, Emily, is my dad available?"

"He's in the shower. Shall I tell him to call you when he gets out?"

"Yes, please. I had a bad night last night. Rick thinks I'm crazy."

"Oh, Tanya, I'm so sorry. Has the thing with your keys gotten worse?"

"I saw something last night, an apparition-like thing...something white but insubstantial. I guess I'm hallucinating. I guess I'm losing my mind." She started to cry.

"Tell me the specifics," I said, buying time and hoping Bud would come out of bathroom to take her call.

"It was just a form at the foot of my bed. It whispered inside my head. It said I'd taken a life and now it was my turn to die. I woke Rick, but by then, it had gone." She started sobbing and hiccuping.

I motioned to Bud as he came out of the bathroom. Covering the phone with my hand, I told him it was Tanya and she was very upset. He took the phone from me, and I listened as he tried to soothe her and told her he'd be right over to see her.

"You'll be alright, honey. Fix yourself a cup of coffee. I'll stop for donuts and come see you. Alright? Will you be okay while I do that?

She must have agreed because Bud then hung up.

"Do you think she's ill?" I asked.

"Don't encourage her," he said sharply to me. I was immediately hurt. I'd just been trying to get her to focus and calm down. But

I didn't want to argue with him, so I said, "I hope you can help her."

"I'll try," he said curtly and hurried out of the room while still pulling his shirt over his head. I heard him grab his keys and go out the door—leaving me without a kiss good-bye. I don't think he'd ever done that before.

I called home several times to find out how Tanya was, but Bud didn't answer the phone.

After work, I drove into Swansea for my appointment with Orvus Kennedy. It wasn't too hard finding a parking spot in Swansea at seven o'clock on a Tuesday evening. Most businesses were closed; the downtown nightlife didn't start until Thursday evening.

Kennedy's office was a restored town house that sat on High Street with many other similarly renovated townhomes referred to by the locals as Lawyer's Row.

The homes were brick, and their front wall sat right on the street without the softening benefit of lawns or front porches. The sidewalk was a herringboned pattern of old bricks, carefully maintained to keep the colonial feel of the neighborhood.

Three marble steps led directly from the sidewalk to the front door; his was painted black with a shiny brass plate bearing the name "Orvus Kennedy, Esquire." I pushed the black doorbell button embedded in the door frame, turned the brass door handle, and walked in.

"Back here," a baritone voice called, so I made my way down a dark hall, past an empty waiting area off to the left, and continued down to the end, where a narrow door opened on my right that led me into the office itself.

Orvus rose from his chair to greet me—a tall, slim man in his forties, with a wide friendly face topped by Kennedyesque brown hair parted on the right and swept to one side. He was very handsome, much more so than the greasy, cheap-suited ambulance chaser I'd been expecting.

He extended his hand for shaking, which I shook, and announced himself as "Orvus Kennedy, at your service." His gold-brown eyes twinkled with the hint of a flirt. I was taken in immediately.

"Thanks for seeing me," I said. "I'd like to say up front that I'm ready to pay your fee for our meeting today. I don't visit lawyers very often, so I'm not really sure of the protocol."

"We personal injury attorneys don't usually charge for the first consultation, so put your mind at rest. Take as much time as you like. You're my last appointment for the day."

Well, that relaxed me. This wasn't going to be a rush job like visiting the doctor who always has a waiting room full of people anxious to be the next person examined.

I sat back, crossed my legs, and took a deep breath, noticing the expensive wood paneling and furniture. There were tall wood filing cabinets and a scattering of glass-topped tables, mostly empty except for an ashtray and a box of Kleenex. The brocade-covered sofa looked very comfortable.

"I'm here to see you about Rose Hamlin," I began. "I understand you saw her five years ago. The night before she died actually. Do you remember her?" We had touched on this briefly on the phone, but repeating it now seemed a good way to get things started.

Orvus opened up a slim manila folder sitting in front of him on the desk.

"I do remember her, although we only met the one time. She was quite upset. She was very articulate...and very attractive. A hard combination to forget. I also have this." He held up an enlarged photocopy of Rosie's driver's license. "I always get a copy of this for many reasons, not the least of which was that she came to see me about a traffic accident. Always good policy to verify the information provided by the client."

"And you know that she's dead?"

"Yes. I tried to call her at work a week or two later, and one of the store employees told me she'd died of a heart attack. I was never contacted by any family members, so as far as I know I'm free to discuss her case with you."

"Thank you. To my knowledge she only had one sister, and that sister didn't give me an address or phone number, so I'm thinking no one else is interested in investigating Rosie's death. But I was her friend for five years, and I knew a little of her family history... Her parents lived until their eighties or nineties, so I just don't think her death was a natural occurrence. She was too young, too healthy. There was no family history of heart disease."

"How did you meet her?" he asked.

"In traffic court. We were both challenging our traffic tickets. Mine was for speeding, and hers was for running a stop sign. We were waiting for our names to be called to go in and see the judge.

"She asked me why I was there and I told her. Then she asked why I was challenging my ticket. I told her there wasn't a sign posted with the speed limit, so I didn't know what the limit was. I thought the limit on an unmarked two-lane road was fifty miles per hour. She thought that was funny. She said it's really thirty-five miles per hour. Her opinion was that I didn't have a prayer of beating it.

"So then I asked her why she was challenging her ticket. She said the police officer who pulled her over had been giving a ticket to another driver when he allegedly saw her roll through the stop sign. She said she had stopped and that he didn't look up until she was pulling away. I thought she had a good argument.

"Rosie's case was called first. She was in there about twenty minutes, then she came out with a big smile on her face...she'd won! I was next, and I lost, of course. When I came out, Rosie was still there and, seeing my face, said she wanted to cheer me up by buying me lunch. So we went to this little deli she knew around the corner from the courthouse. We had such a good time, what with her mimicking the judge and the old cop, that I forgot about having to pay a huge fine for going fifteen miles over the speed limit. After that day, we were friends."

The attorney looked thoughtful. "I got a sense from Rose that she didn't have many friends or didn't keep her friends for long. Was that true?"

"Well, yes. She was easily offended, and she overreacted to criticism. In fact, sometimes her behavior was downright irrational. I remember one time we were at dinner and I excused myself to go to the ladies' room. When I got back, Rosie was putting on her coat and preparing to leave, even though we hadn't finished our entrees. I asked her what was wrong and she said, 'You wouldn't understand. In fact, you don't even *try* to understand. There are books out there about people with my problems. You haven't even read them.'

"I told her I wasn't aware that she had problems. That she'd never talked to me about them. She didn't respond to that, she just threw some money on the table for her share of the bill and walked off. The next time she called she acted as if the whole scene hadn't happened. After that, I learned to walk on eggshells when I was with her. I never challenged her thinking or disagreed with anything she said."

"That must have been difficult," Orvus said.

"Well, I was used to it. My father had such a bad temper that you were always careful not to say anything that would set him off. But he was also a warm, loving, intelligent man, and I felt that way about Rosie too. So she wasn't perfect...Who is? Her good points far outweighed her bad. And she always listened to my problems with a sympathetic ear. I really enjoyed her company most of the time.

"In the five years we were friends, I saw her make and lose friends along the way. She also had boyfriends here and there, but they never lasted. The longest-lasting relationship she had was with a guy named Derek. I've wondered if he had anything to do with her death. I have talked to him about it, though, and I don't think he did anything to hurt her. Maybe he broke her heart, but it would have happened a year or so before she died. What do you think?"

I purposefully left out everything about my paranormal experiences and my joining the SRBPS investigation. I didn't want him to think I was just another flake.

"Why are you looking into this now...five years later?"

"I recently found a bag of her old clothes, and it got me thinking about her and how she died." Again, I didn't want to say I had recently seen her. I'd had enough men dismiss me as a fool.

"Do you know if there was ever any physical violence from the boyfriend?" Orvus asked.

"The police say no, and I'd have to agree. I saw some of the autopsy photos. There were no injuries or deep bruises."

"How did you get autopsy photos?"

"A friend." I chose to leave it at that, not wanting to get anyone in trouble.

"Well, I've never heard of anyone really dying of a broken heart," Orvus said. "Had she lost a lot of weight and been very depressed after the breakup?

"No, not really. She was pretty tough physically and mentally. She rarely went to the doctor. That's why her death strikes me as so odd. I really don't think there was anyone else who knew her as well as I did. I was the one Rosie called the day she died when she felt ill. I was the one who discovered her body. I was the one who called 9-1-1 and administered CPR until the ambulance got there. I've just never been able to get it into my head that she died of a heart attack with no other contributing factors."

"She didn't say anything to you before she died?"

"No, I'm afraid not."

The lawyer sat back for a moment and eyed me with that is-this-client-crazy look. I thought it would add to my credibility to be quiet for a moment, so we sat there silently looking at each other for maybe ten seconds.

"What do you want me to do?" he finally asked.

"I want you to tell me why Rosie called you, what happened when she had the car accident. Is it possible she suffered internal injuries that led to the heart attack? And more importantly, why did she want to hire you?"

"Well, as I recall, she thought she'd been set up. I was reviewing my notes, and here's what she said happened: Her car was stopped at a red light, waiting to make a left-hand turn. A police car came up behind her and bumped into the rear of her car, jolting her. She was shocked, at first, and surprised that a police car would hit her. It wasn't a hard hit, it only jostled her. She looked in her rearview mirror and saw an officer jump out of the police car and come running up to her car. Rose got out, and the police officer said, 'Why did you hit me?'

"Rose explained that the police car had hit *her*. The officer then said that no, the police car had come to a full stop, and then Rose had backed into it. The officer pointed to a dent in the front bumper of the police car and told her she had caused that damage. Rose was angry. She told me she knew she hadn't done what she had been accused of doing. She told me she said to the officer, 'You're not going to get away with this. You better call your superior officer and get someone out here to look at this. There's no damage to my car. I know that I didn't damage yours.' She said the officer replied, 'This is between you and me. I'm writing you a ticket. You're going to appear in court, and your insurance company will be billed for the repair of my vehicle.' I'm afraid Rose didn't react well to what the police officer said.

"I told her I'd heard of the police pulling this sort of operation before. They get to charge a civilian with damaging their vehicles when, in actuality, they are responsible and don't want it on their record."

"What did Rosie do?"

"She lost her temper. By this time the red light had changed to green and any cars that might have witnessed the event had driven off. Rosie started shouting that the officer wasn't going to get away with it and she'd sue. She'd call her congressman and she'd have this woman's job."

"This woman?"

"Oh yes, the police officer was female. She was a tall woman, Rose said, easily six feet. And she became enraged when she saw that Rose wasn't going to accept her version of events."

The description was a familiar one. I didn't want to think about who the officer might be. Hadn't Tanya said there were other women on the force?

"Then what happened?" I asked.

"Unfortunately, Rose said she took a swing at her."

"Oh no, and then what? Was she arrested?"

"No, she only received a ticket, but not before the police officer took out her Taser and discharged it into Rose's abdomen."

"Oh no! I can only imagine how much that hurt. Rosie was a tiny person. That police officer totally overreacted." I was shocked, but now I had an explanation for the marks on Rosie's shirt and torso.

"Rose calmed down after that. Getting tasered stuns you for a few minutes. You can feel dizzy and confused. Some people feel pain, but it dissipates quickly. I think the shock to your dignity is worse than the actual sting of the Taser."

"Do you think the shock of the Taser could have brought on Rosie's heart attack?" I asked.

"It's possible. I've done some research, and there's evidence to support it. It's not a clear-cut result, but there are documented cases of Tasers causing heart arrhythmia and subsequent heart attacks and death."

I was silent, thinking, and the more I thought about it, the more certain I was that this was the cause of Rosie's death. Why else would a forty-seven-year-old woman with no family history of heart trouble die of a heart attack? I had my answer at last. It also meant Derek hadn't killed her.

Orvus continued, "She let the officer write her a ticket and then called me as soon as she got back to work and briefly explained what had happened and asked me to start the paperwork for filing a lawsuit against the Swansea police. We met that night, talked about the details, and I told her I'd do it."

"Poor Rosie. What a crummy thing to have happen to her. So I guess you never filed the suit. Too bad. That officer should be punished."

"I could still file a complaint if you'd like me to. It's not the same as a lawsuit...there won't be a hearing...but it will go on her record. This is a small town, people talk, everyone will know eventually and she'll suffer a lot of shame in the community."

"Let's do it. How do you file a complaint?"

"I just have to write a letter to the chief of police stating the details of the event and that you're requesting further investigation of the officer."

"Fine, I'm all for it. Do you have the name of the officer?"

"Yes, it's here in the file. Tanya Dresser."

"Oh no." My worst fear was confirmed.

"What?"

"My boyfriend is Bud O'Doul. Tanya is his daughter."

"Tough call," Orvus said and sat back in his chair, disengaging for a moment so we could each reconsider.

"I know Bud," he finally said after a few moments. "I like him. And I know his daughter. I think she has a spotless record so far."

The bigger question for me now was how would I tell Bud that his daughter had caused the death of my best friend?

I sighed. "How can we let police officers go around tasering people willy-nilly and possibly causing their death? It's outrageous. It shouldn't be allowed. Could Tanya be charged with murder?"

"Do you really want to do that?" Orvus said, sounding shocked. "Taser use is an accepted police procedure. I don't think you'd win, and you might become a target yourself."

He had a point. I needed to think about this carefully.

He was quiet for a moment and then added, "I hear what you're saying about the Taser, but the alternatives are the billy club or the service revolver. Not good options. I understand the dilemma the police are in."

"But the bottom line is that a trained, physically fit, six-foot-tall police officer should have taken some other action to subdue a tiny, mouthy woman rather than shooting her with a Taser. If it's not murder, it's at least excessive force."

"We weren't there, Emily. We don't know what went on. In the officer's defense, I asked Rose if she had a gun or threatened to produce a gun. She said no."

"I don't think she owned a gun," I said. "Or even mace or pepper spray. Even though she lived alone and traveled a lot, she never mentioned carrying anything to protect herself. So I don't think she would have threatened the officer with anything except her fists."

"Well, what would you like to do?" Orvus was still sitting back in his chair, not in a hurry for a decision. He was probably thinking I needed time to calm down. I was thinking I'd need to sleep on it.

"I have to think about all this," I said. "I'll call you."

"Think carefully," he replied. "Bud won't take this well."

Didn't I know it.

Chapter Twenty-One

When I left the office, I looked at my watch. It was eight thirty. Not too late, really, to knock on someone's door. Tanya had arrived unannounced at my front door. I felt free to arrive unannounced at hers.

It crossed my mind that going to see her was a bad idea. I knew for sure that Bud would not approve. But, at some point in a relationship, you just get tired of always altering your behavior because of what your significant other might or might not approve of. I wanted to confront Tanya personally, like the police do, knocking on her door without warning.

Bud had told me she lived on the other side of Swansea, near Route 10, closer to Keene. I figured I could find her address. Swansea was not that big a town.

After turning at one of two shopping centers and following what looked like a well-traveled thoroughfare, I found the cross street, West Summit. About six blocks in, I found 514, a brick Cape Cod with brown trim. A black Ford Explorer and a Swansea Police Department car sat in the driveway.

The living room windows were open; white sheers moved gently in the warm evening breeze. As I got out of my car, I could hear people arguing. I stood in the shadow of their house and listened.

"Don't you care whether or not I'm seeing things and hearing things and experiencing things I can't explain?"

"You're making too big a deal of this, Tanya. Life is full of things we can't explain. You don't see me losing any sleep over it, do you?"

"You don't lose sleep over anything, Rick. The roof is leaking, the kitchen drainpipe is stopped up, and half the doors in this house don't shut properly. Don't you care how you live? Don't you care that things should work well and perform like they should? You have no standards, no standards at all! I'm the one who has all the responsibility." She continued in a shrill voice. "I'm the one who has to call the repairmen and do the laundry and buy the groceries and see that the bills are paid. Why don't you do any of these things?"

"You know I would if you'd just give me a chance. The problem is that you always want them done yesterday. I'd get around to doing them eventually."

"No you wouldn't. The last time I was sick and asked you to pay the bills we nearly lost our electricity."

"That was one time. One time. You're too picky. Relax. Enjoy life. Then these weird things will stop happening to you. Have a glass of wine. Put your feet up. Take it easy."

"You sound just like my father, and he's a drunk! He ran off and left my mom to raise me all alone. He sent a check every month, but when did he come by to see me? Once a year. Once a year at Christmas. That was my father. Is that the kind of person you think I should be? Is it?"

"Do you think we should get divorced?"

It came out of the dark, angry night like gunfire. Bang! Bang! The marriage was dead. He wanted out. He had just been waiting for a chance to say it.

"Okay," she said, defeated. She sounded as if she had known this was coming. Then there was silence, except for the whir of the katydids, the sound track of summer.

I needed to sit down and sank onto the edge of their brick porch. I was struck to the heart by Rick's words, the exact same words my husband had said to me more than ten years earlier as we sat in our car arguing outside of a friend's house, too upset and angry to go in and join them for a game of cards. He had said "Do you think we should get divorced?" and I had been Tanya, arguing for what was right, fighting for a home where I would feel loved, hoping for a relationship where my values were respected.

He left me—so he would be free to let the dirty dishes sit in the sink, free to pay the electric bill the day before shutoff, and free to let his house fall down around him if that's what suited him. He did not take even one photograph of us with him when he left.

No way could I knock on Tanya's door. I could barely walk back to my car. As I drove home, I pulled into a shopping center and parked where there were no other cars. I put my face in my hands, my forehead against the steering wheel, and cried. I cried for myself, for Tanya, for all of us who struggle to find love and acceptance and then, when we think we've found it, have it pulled out from under us by those seven awful words.

When I was sobbed out, I continued my drive home, consumed with thoughts of my new relationship with Bud and the accusations leveled by his daughter. Is this the man I wanted to spend the rest of my life with, a man who would leave his wife and ignore his child? I didn't know the details of his marriage, but Tanya had made it pretty clear that she didn't blame her mother. But Bud was older and wiser now, I argued with myself. His daughter was welcome in our home any time. He was always glad to speak to her on the phone. I, personally, had never seen him drunk. People *could* change.

I also realized that it would hurt him terribly for Orvus to initiate any action against his daughter. It would end our relationship, and in my dating experience, he was one of the most wonderful men I'd ever met. We had talked about marriage, with Bud being the more eager of us, and my being the one with cold feet.

Tanya was his only child. I couldn't hurt him. I couldn't risk losing him.

When I got home, Bud had saved me a plate of roast chicken and green beans. I didn't bring up the topic of his daughter. He asked how the meeting with Orvus had gone and why I was so quiet. I said I didn't want to talk about the meeting and that I didn't feel well, which wasn't a lie. I was sick at heart.

But I did get up the courage to ask him about the incident with Rosie's car. "When you were on the police force, did you ever hear of a scam where a car hits the car in front of it on purpose, and then claims the other driver backed into the car behind it and caused damage to their vehicle? Damage that had been caused in a previous accident."

"I've heard of it. But I don't know of anyone who ever tried it. Why do you ask?"

"Orvus Kennedy and I were talking about it. He said even police officers have been known to do it to cover up accidents with their patrol cars."

"That's nonsense," he replied, then angrily grabbed my empty plate along with his and took our dishes out to the kitchen. I could hear him rinsing them off and putting them in the dishwasher, banging the door shut. I didn't pursue it.

We watched TV for a little while and then went to bed. I was feeling out of sorts and Bud could tell, but he didn't press me for an explanation. I fell asleep wondering when the pain of a broken marriage went away. Did it ever? My anger at Tanya for causing the death of my friend was all mixed up with my sympathy for what she was going through on her job and in her marriage. Why did it have to be so complicated?

I finally fell asleep and dreamt of malls with mannequins in police uniforms. The stores were closed and all the shoppers were wandering around lost and alone, waiting for the stores to open.

Chapter Twenty-Two: Wednesday

On Wednesday I spent the workday monitoring the trainees, with special attention to Grace. She still hadn't caught on to simultaneously speaking to customers and using the computer to draw up their account information. Behind her back, Pat gave me a sad shake of her head. Even Pat thought she wasn't doing well enough to keep the job.

Around lunchtime I got a call from Melinda.

"The guys are here with the results of their investigation of Old Stone Mill. I think you'll be interested. Want to come over after dinner?"

Would I? Something to take my mind off my dilemma. I told her I'd be there around seven.

Bud had prepared his famous barbecued shrimp dinner with french fries and coleslaw. I declined a glass of wine and told him about going to see Melinda. He seemed a little hurt that I was leaving so soon after getting home, but I knew it'd be awkward for me to sit and watch TV with him and pretend that nothing was wrong.

Melinda had a perfect little bungalow out in the sticks. It was a one-story log cabin with a wide porch stretching along the west-facing front, and a huge stone fireplace dominating the north side. You could sit on her porch, as I had done many times, and watch the sun set in all its pink, gold, and lavender splendor behind the snow-capped White Mountains of New Hampshire. After the sun set, we'd go inside and get cozy with vodka-infused hot chocolate, savored on her comfy green plaid couch before a roaring fire.

This being June, there was just a small blaze going in the hearth illuminating the silver laptop that sat on the nearby dining room table. Melinda, James, and Ed—one of the SRBPS technicians—were seated there, each enjoying a beer.

"What did you get?" I asked right away.

"You'll love it," Melinda replied. "Can I get you an Allagash?"

"Please, it's been a tough day."

I took a seat at the table and nodded a hello to the guys.

Ed began, "I've been reviewing all the DVR and EVP evidence with Melinda, and you were a witness to most of what we have. We're very excited to have caught the levitation of objects in Derek's condo. I don't think there's anything quite like it in all recorded paranormal history. There were just two things you missed."

Ed reached for his laptop and brought up footage of the front entrance of the condo building just prior to my team's starting out to investigate.

For just a brief few seconds, a figure appeared in the doorway, a small featureless ghost looking dainty and female. There was a lonely mournfulness to her that I couldn't explain. Then she disappeared.

"Who was that?" I asked.

"We don't know," Ed answered. "It could have been your friend, or it could have been one of the many mill workers who died there over the mill's two-hundred-year history. We also have this."

He accessed a file labeled "EVP 6.02.2000...04:05:25."

"This was recorded when we were in Derek's condo. You'll hear the sound of the Star Trek figures as they hit the floor. Underneath it, there's a voice. Tell me what you hear."

James clicked on Start, and immediately I heard the crashing of toys as they landed on the floor and one of the crew asking the cameraman, "Are you getting this?"

Then softly, in a whisper almost not to be heard, was a voice saying, "Get her...get her...get her."

"It's saying 'Get *her*, not get *him*, right?" I asked.

"That's what it sounds like to us." Melinda agreed.

"So are we to think that Rosie is haunting Derek's apartment but telling us to punish a woman? That doesn't make sense."

"I can't answer that," Melinda said. "It's possible that he's more receptive to paranormal experiences, or that Rosie is having problems getting through to you. I don't really know."

"I haven't had a chance to tell you about this, Melinda, but Orvus Kennedy told me last night that, on the day before she died, Rosie was tasered by a police officer...a woman police officer...the one you met at my house."

"Bud's daughter!"

"Yes. What am I going to do? Rosie had planned to sue her; that's why she went to see a lawyer. It's a long story, but basically Tanya was pulling a scam on her and Rosie wouldn't cooperate. When Rosie got angry, Tanya used a Taser on her to get her to calm down. Rosie died the next day of a heart attack. I think the Taser caused an arrhythmia in Rosie's heart and that's why she had the heart attack. In my book, Tanya killed her. I told Orvus to prepare a letter of complaint to the Swansea Police Department."

"Wait a minute," broke in James. "We don't have any definite proof that the spirit who was interacting with us was your friend. This evidence is in no way admissible in court. You may be jumping to conclusions, and a policewoman's career is at stake. I agree that what you're saying is plausible, but I wouldn't take any action based on it."

I sighed. James was absolutely right. Was I misinterpreting events? Did I sound like a crazy woman taking instructions from the spirit world? As compelling as all this was, I couldn't wreck Tanya's life, or Bud's, or mine, based on paranormal phenomena. Maybe the Taser had caused Rosie's death, but there was really nothing I could do about it. Maybe Rosie's heart attack had nothing to do with the Taser shock. The evidence was just not strong enough to go forward with any type of legal action.

"You're right," I acknowledged. "Thank you, though, for letting me go with you on your investigation. What are you going to tell the residents?"

"I don't know," James said. "I need to think about it. No one other than Derek and Martha has reported objects being moved. Maybe it was a show just for our benefit. And maybe now that the spirits have communicated with us, they'll go back to being quiet."

"Have you shown all this to Derek and Martha?"

"Tomorrow night."

"Thank you, all," I said and got up to leave. "I'll call you," I said, nodding to Melinda. I was so tired now. I couldn't wait to get home and go to bed.

Chapter Twenty-Three

Bud was asleep when I let myself in around ten thirty. I went through my usual nightly routine of brushing my teeth, washing my face, and applying face cream. As I climbed into bed between him and Casey, I sighed with contentment. How could I even imagine taking the risk of losing my wonderful little family?

Bud turned over and said, "How'd it go?"

"They caught some interesting voice phenomena," I said. I hadn't fully told Bud what had gone on in the investigation. I knew he didn't believe any of it.

"What did the voices say?"

"The voice said, 'Get her.' I don't know what that means...Bud, is Tanya really alright? How did she seem today?"

I was anxious to change the topic and not start a fight about paranormal phenomena.

"She's worse. She's believing all that nonsense that you believe about spirit voices and being haunted. I can't understand why she puts any faith in that garbage."

It didn't sound as if she'd mentioned the divorce to her dad.

"Maybe it would help her resolve her problem if she took it seriously. I mean in the sense that she's done something wrong that needs to be made right." This was the closest I could come to suggesting Tanya was at fault for Rosie's death.

"That's it!" Bud shouted, getting out of bed. Stunned at his reaction, I sat there silently as he put on the shorts and shirt he'd left by the bed earlier in the evening. Then he put on his sandals and stood up.

"I'm going to apartment," he said. "I can't deal with you and your stupid theories any longer. C'mon Casey, let's go."

Bud started for the bedroom door and turned to make sure that Casey was following him.

Casey didn't even attempt to rouse himself from his soft warm spot on the bed next to me. I smiled to myself.

"Damn it, come on," Bud said, standing in the doorway.

Casey didn't move.

Bud walked downstairs without Casey following. I heard him moving around in the kitchen. He called up again,

"Casey, let's go!"

Casey didn't budge.

I smiled and snuggled down in the covers. I patted my champion on the head. "I love you too," I whispered to him.

I lay there for about twenty minutes, waiting to hear Bud go out the door, which he never did. Then I fell asleep. The next morning, I found Bud asleep on the sofa.

I didn't wake him as I let Casey out, prepared for work, let Casey back in, and sat down to eat some cereal.

I found my lunch on the counter already packed. I could see a little note wrapped around the crackers. Bud often tucked a love note in my lunch, just a short message saying something like "Love ya!" It always touched my heart. This note had a heart drawn on it with one word written inside it, "Sorry."

"See you around five thirty," I whispered as I kissed his sleeping face good-bye.

It was a good sign he'd stayed. Maybe we could make a go of this yet.

When I got to work, my friend Pat was looking for me.

"Grace was fired this morning," she told me.

"How did she take it?"

"Lots of tears. It wasn't pretty. I just wanted you to know before you saw Joan."

"Thanks, Pat." It seemed like a bad omen. I had to remember to call Orvus and tell him definitely not to write a complaint letter.

I sat down at my desk just in time to see Joan leave her office and head in my direction with a stack of papers in her hand. She looked worried. I'd expected her to look smug.

"Fire drill," she said when she got within hearing. She made no mention of Grace.

"Corporate has come out with new security procedures for the whole call center. You'll need to start training immediately. Every rep must be trained by end of day."

"Here are the new guidelines," she said, waving the papers in her hands. "All the reps will now need to verify three pieces of a caller's personal information instead of two. It's effective immediately."

Joan handed me the pages of instruction and turned to leave.

"Oh, by the way," she said, as she stalked back to her office, looking back at me briefly, "Grace is gone."

She wasn't interested in my response, so I gave none. My call to Orvus would have to wait until later.

When I took a break at one thirty, having trained twelve of our twenty pods of representatives, I sat down at my desk and dialed the lawyer's number. I wasn't happy to get his voice mail. I left a message that he shouldn't write the letter we had discussed and that I'd call him tomorrow. Then I gobbled down my lunch, pocketed Bud's note, and headed back to the floor.

At five o'clock I collapsed at my desk. The training had been easy enough with a minimum of questions, but it had been tedious and, toward the end, boring. You can only repeat the same information so many times without getting tired of hearing yourself talk. With dismay, I noticed the message light blinking on my phone. Wearily I dialed the voice mail.

"Emily, it's Melinda. Bad news. Can you meet me at Shenanigan's for a quick drink right after work? I need to talk to you about something in person."

I deleted her message, but there was a second voice mail from Orvus.

"Very sorry," his voice began. "I didn't hear from you yesterday, so I gave my notes to my legal assistant to file. I guess she took a look at them.

"I didn't know my assistant had gone to high school with Tanya Dresser. Unfortunately, she thought she needed to alert her about your complaint. Tanya didn't take it well. Please call me as soon as you get this message. It's urgent."

Could this day get any worse?

I called Bud to tell him I'd be late, but there was no answer. Then I called Orvus, but his line was busy. Then I called Melinda back and it rang six times before switching to her voice mail, meaning she was out. I was sweating by now and had a bad feeling in the pit of my stomach. Too many people were unavailable all at the same time. It was a bad sign.

I left a message for Melinda, "On my way."

I was just locking up my desk when Joan appeared. What now? I thought.

"Can I see you for just a moment in my office?"

"Of course," I said and got up to follow her. Was this the ax?

Once in her office, Joan sat behind her desk and opened a manila folder. I sat on the edge of the chair opposite her.

"I'm sorry we had to let Grace go."

I didn't believe her.

"Yes," was all I said. Nothing could be done now.

"Well, I do have some good news for you. It has come to Metrobank's attention that when Sussex County Savings and Loan was acquired, its trainers were paid less than those at Metrobank. Legally, we're required to correct that. It's necessary to raise your salary 4.5 percent effective July 1st."

Such good news! And yet she said it as if it pained her. I had to smile. I needed every penny of that raise.

"Please sign this acknowledgment that we've had this conversation," she continued, pushing a paper across her desk to me accompanied by a black ballpoint pen.

"I'll be glad to...and thank you," I replied. Might as well be gracious, and then hopefully I could run out the door.

I quickly signed on the line Joan had marked with a tiny "x" and rose to leave.

"This doesn't change anything," she added.

"I understand," I replied, but I said it with a smile. I was happy whether she wanted me to be or not. Maybe this was a good omen and my day was about to get better.

Luckily Melinda had picked a bar just one shopping center over from the Metrobank office complex. I parked my little Honda Civic and practically ran into the building. I saw Melinda in a corner booth, her head bowed solemnly, staring at the table. There was a glass of white wine already waiting for me.

She stood up and hugged me, then said "Sit down, take a breath, and have a sip or two. I don't have good news."

"Okay," I said, wondering what could be so bad. Had something happened to Bud? But then she would have met me at the hospital, not at a bar.

After two sips and a couple of deep breaths, I put down my

glass and said "What's happened?"

"Have you heard from Bud?" she asked.

"No. I tried to call, but he didn't answer."

"Tanya's in the hospital as the result of a gunshot wound. It's on the news that she tried to kill herself."

"Oh no, poor Tanya! Poor Bud! Why didn't he call me and tell me?" Feelings erupted inside me; I was scared and horrified at this turn of events.

"I don't know why Bud didn't call. If you hadn't shown up, I'd have figured Bud did call you and you were with him. But here you are."

Yes, here I was. Why hadn't Bud called?

"Oh, what a mess. I had to train all day and couldn't make any phone calls until lunchtime. When I did call Orvus, I had to leave a message. Then I got a phone message from him saying his legal assistant might have tipped Tanya off to my complaint."

I felt sick to my stomach with panic and grief. I crossed my arms across my waist and started to rock back and forth.

"Well, I guess his assistant must have told Tanya about what you were planning to do. The story being reported is that she phoned her father, threatening suicide. Bud drove to her house and found her already lying on the floor with a self-inflicted gunshot wound to the head. She left a suicide note saying someone, the news is not naming anyone, had destroyed her career."

Could there be anything more horrible? What had I done? While I had been stuck at the bank, Bud had almost lost his only child, all because of that wretched Rosie sucking me into her plan for revenge. Or had she? Could everything have been my overactive imagination?

Or could the divorce have been the final straw to push Tanya over the edge?

"I have to go home," I told Melinda. "I have to see if Bud is there or if he left a note."

"Of course."

As I rose to leave, a thought occurred to me. "Did you know this was going to happen? Did you sense it?"

"No, Em, I'm sorry. I didn't."

She was my friend. I chose to believe her.

I ran out of the bar, got in my car, and sped toward home. Why hadn't Bud tried to call? Or did he blame me and didn't want to see me? I felt so guilty. It briefly crossed my mind to drive directly to the hospital, but if Bud didn't want me there, I didn't want to cause him any more pain. And if he did blame me, I didn't think I could face him. I had to check the house first. Maybe he'd left a note.

When I pulled into my driveway and got out of my car, I almost threw up—that's how ill I felt. I was dizzy with fear. I lurched up the front walk.

When I opened the door, there was no Casey to greet me. The house was eerily silent. I looked quickly in the kitchen, living room, and dining room. No Bud, no Casey, no note.

I ran up the stairway and into our bedroom. The first thing I noticed was the nightstand swept clean of Bud's personal effects and medications. I opened the closet, and his side was empty. As was the dresser drawer where he'd kept his socks and underwear.

I looked everywhere for a note, but couldn't find one.

I sat on the bed and cried—and cried, and then cried some more—until I had no tears and no hope left in me. I curled up in the fetal position, pulled the covers over me, and prayed to God and all the angels for help. "Don't let Tanya die," I begged over and over again.

Should I go to the hospital anyway, without Bud's asking? I decided no. Since he'd moved his things out, it would seem that he blamed me for Tanya's suicide attempt. It was obvious, he not only didn't want me at the hospital, he didn't want me at all anymore. My presence would only upset him further.

I felt as if my life were over. As if there were no way that I could move forward from this spot. I was consumed with pain—pain for Tanya, pain for Bud—and anger at myself for being such a stupid twit.

I prayed again that Tanya would survive without any loss of brain function and that she would be able to resume her life. I wanted to pray for Bud, but couldn't. He blamed me totally for a situation I wouldn't have wanted to happen. But I did pray that someday, somehow, we could be friends and lovers again.

Chapter Twenty-Four

I slept, willfully and gratefully descending into a deep pit of forgetfulness. I awoke to a gray morning and went immediately to the phone to call Bud at his apartment. There was no answer.

I put down the receiver and thought about calling the hospital to ask about Tanya. Then the phone rang. Bud! Please, let it be Bud.

"Hello?" I whispered.

"Hey, Em, it's Derek. How's it hanging?"

He was not the person I wanted to speak to this morning.

"What do you want, Derek?"

"Don't be pissy, Em. I wanted you to know that everything has stopped."

"Stopped?"

"No mist on my bed last night. No things moving around. I woke up and the whole place just felt lighter and cleaner somehow."

"I'm glad, Derek. So why are you calling me?"

"Well, I'm not done yet. When I got out of the shower this morning there was the usual condensation on the mirror, but there was a word spelled out in the mist on the glass. It was B-Y-E, 'BYE.' Whoever or whatever was bothering me was saying good-bye. Whatever you guys did when you were here, it worked. It's gone. I just wanted you to know."

If nothing else, this confirmed that Rosie's unhappy spirit had been responsible for everything that had happened.

"That's great, Derek. I've got to go. Thanks for calling."

"No problem. And, Em, if you ever feel like getting together for a drink again, just call. I enjoyed talking to you the other day," and with that he hung up. Wow, everything about that call had been a poorly timed surprise.

Before anyone else could call me, I dialed Melinda's number.

She answered on the first ring, as if expecting my call.

"Melinda, it's Emily. When I got home last night, Bud had moved out all his things. He's not answering his phone. I guess he's still at the hospital sitting with Tanya. Have you heard anything?"

"I have a friend who works there and gave me news. I'm afraid Tanya died last night. I was waiting until I thought you were up to call you. I'm so sorry. This is a tragedy I could never have imagined."

"It's all Rosie's fault," I said and then told her about Derek's phone call. I also told her about Tanya's divorce. "Will Rosie be satisfied with the damage she's done?" I asked.

"You knew her better than I. What do you think?"

"I hope so. There's been enough heartache to go around to fulfill anyone's desire for revenge. Bud will never believe that Rosie's ghost haunted his daughter. He's going to go on living with the thought that Tanya was mentally unstable. It couldn't get much sadder. He won't have anything more to do with me now. Oh, Melinda, how do I go forward from this? I loved that man so much. And now his daughter is dead, he blames me, and he's gone from my life."

"Stay home from work today, Em. Take it easy. Watch old movies. Let yourself be numb. The days will slide by, and without your even knowing it, this ocean of sorrow that you're drowning in will shrink into a sad little creek that only bubbles up now and then to remind you of where you've been. But you'll gather strength from it too. It's not the water of death, Em, it's the water of life." Melinda, the psychic, was telling me that Bud wasn't coming back.

"I'll try," I said. "But I don't think I'll ever be able to forgive myself."

After leaving a message on Joan's answering machine that I was taking a sick day, I climbed back under the covers and pulled them up around me. Then I closed my eyes and tried to convince my brain that Bud was not gone forever.

Chapter Twenty-Five

I spent the entire weekend in bed, alternately sleeping and watching the Home and Garden channel on TV. Seeing old walls ripped down, floors replaced, and shiny new appliances installed made me momentarily forget my loneliness and self-accusatory thoughts.

That weekend will forever be remembered as the longest one in my life. I missed bringing Bud breakfast and cuddling with him as we watched the news. I missed Casey's warm presence beside me in bed. I missed Bud's voice and his huge personality overshadowing everything I did.

There was no one else's comfort to be concerned with, except my own, and that made me feel useless. I worried that Bud would be so overwhelmed with grief that he would forget to take his medications.

All day Saturday I was sure Bud would call. With every breath, I listened for the ring of the phone. He never called. By Sunday evening, I knew he never would.

I thought about whether I should attend Tanya's funeral service, but out of respect for Bud, it seemed best if I didn't.

On Monday I returned to work. My training class was officially over, and I would now set about devising measurements to see how well my students performed two, four, and six weeks out from training.

I wanted to say something to Joan about calling in sick so suddenly on Friday, but she wasn't in her office. Around three o'clock, I stopped by Pat's desk and asked her if she knew where Joan was.

"Oh, she's in court today. Something about suing the Swansea Police Department for a fraudulent accident at a traffic light."

"That happened to her too? I know someone else who was a victim of that scam."

"Well, she has a pricey Boston lawyer and, given her attitude, I'm betting she wins her case and then some."

"Do you know who the officer was?"

"I think it was more than one. Maybe a woman and two guys."

So Tanya hadn't been in this alone. I wondered how much peer pressure there might have been to join in the ruse. It would have been a way for her to feel like one of the guys.

Then it struck me, perhaps the voices and the divorce hadn't been Tanya's reason for shooting herself. Perhaps it'd been the looming trial and eventual disgrace. Her father had retired from the police force. She would be dismissed.

My talking to Orvus wouldn't have made any difference.

"Thanks, Pat. I'll talk to her later this week. By the way, I don't see Martha here."

"You didn't hear? Well, I guess not, you were out Friday. She up and quit. No reason given. She just walked in at seven thirty and handed in her resignation."

I walked away deep in thought. Martha had been Rosie's friend. The problems at the condo had started right after she moved in with Derek. That phone call I thought was Rosie's voice occurred after she started the training class.

I decided to do something I never thought I'd do. I called Derek.

"Hi, Derek, it's Emily. Do you have a minute?"

"Always for you, babe."

"I know you thought the weird events you experienced in your condo were over Friday, but did anything else happen over the weekend?"

"No, the whole atmosphere is different now. Everything feels light and clean, but Martha and I decided the relationship wasn't working. She was also pretty spooked by that video from the ghost investigators. She moved out Sunday."

"I'm sorry to hear that, but I'm happy the haunting is over. You take care of yourself, and let me know if it starts up again."

"Can't talk you into dinner some Saturday night?"

"I just broke up with someone too. I need a little time to recover."

"Well, just give me a call any time, Em. I'm sure we'll have lots to talk about."

"Thank you, Derek. I just might do that."

I couldn't help but wonder what part Martha had played in all that had happened. Her actions outside the condo couldn't explain everything that had happened inside that night. But perhaps Rosie's jealous spirit is what had started everything.

Martha could have been the person I saw at the Laundromat, and she could have been the voice on the phone, but she couldn't have caused the levitation of objects in the condo. As the investigators always claim, once you've ruled out everything that could have a logical explanation, what's left over is the paranormal, and what happened in Derek's condo was certainly paranormal.

I shut off my PC and decided to sneak out of work a little early. I still needed time to rest and think about what I wanted to do with my future. I would have to replan it all, without Bud and without my beloved Casey. Well, it certainly wasn't my first go round with disappointment.

I had my job, even a raise – and HGTV. Maybe I'd go to the hardware store on Saturday. I would survive.

The End

Author's Note

I have never seen a ghost nor have I been on a ghost investigation, so my description of these activities comes entirely from research and the media. That is not to say I don't believe in ghosts. I am a person open to the possibilities.

Follow the clues with Emily Menotti
as she unravels still more mysteries:

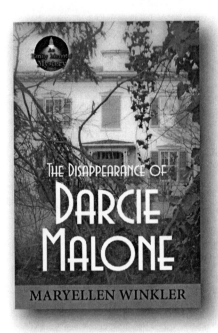

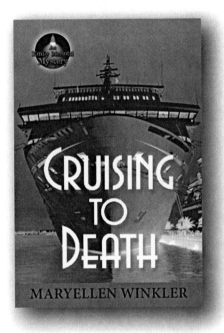

On a warm September night in 1969, a young couple embarks on a romantic midnight picnic on the grounds of a legendary haunted house. By morning, the girl has disappeared, and her boyfriend is found mentally confused and unable to speak. She is never found, and the mystery is never resolved.

Thirty years later, Emily stands in the dark and hears an old man singing, calling out for "Darcie." She turns to see who is singing, but no one's there.

Join Emily as she is drawn deeper into discovering what happened to Darcie Malone.

Intrepid amateur sleuth, Emily Menotti, is on her first Caribbean cruise along with the Wayward Sisters book club. As they head out of New York City, however, a friend goes missing.

With the help of her clairsentient pal, Melinda, Emily starts investigating. Yet even a séance, guided by Melinda, reveals more old secrets than new clues.

Set amid tropical backdrops, this mystery has motives aplenty, including an ex-husband, a former high school boyfriend, and the ongoing resentment of two unmarried friends.

Join Emily as she solves the mystery on a chilling cruise with some uninvited passengers: jealousy, revenge, and death.

CPSIA information can be obtained
at www.ICGtesting.com
Printed in the USA
FSOW01n1404060118
42958FS